ODIN'S GATEWAYS

Published by Avalonia

BM Avalonia
London
WC1N 3XX
England, UK

www.avaloniabooks.co.uk

ODIN's GATEWAYS
Copyright © Katie Gerrard 2009

ISBN-10: 1905297319
ISBN-13: 978-1905297313

First Edition, November 2009
Design by Satori
Cover Art "Odin's Gateways" by Laura Daligan (c) 2009

British Library Cataloguing in Publication Data. A catalogue
record for this book is available from the British Library.

ABOUT THE AUTHOR: KATIE GERRARD

Katie Gerrard is a writer, researcher and workshop facilitator with a passion for the magic of the Runes and Seidr. She has been studying the different forms of Norse magic and working with the Norse Gods since discovering them in the 1990s, when she was at university in West Wales.

Katie lectures and facilitates workshops at national and international events on the Runes, Seidr and related subjects, and also leads a practical Seidr group on the outskirts of London. Her work on the runes spans understanding, divination, voice work, and runic magic, and she is currently teaching courses on this subject from Treadwells Bookshop in Central London (UK). Her work on Seidr focuses on the High Seat rite and her essay 'The Seer' on this subject appeared in the Avalonia anthology *Priestesses, Pythonesses, Sibyls*.

When she is not doing things of a magickal persuasion she enjoys creative pursuits such as fashion design, sewing, and various handicrafts. She lives in London with her husband, daughter, and fat idiot cat.

She is currently engaged in writing her second book which brings together many years of research with experimental work she has done with Seidr techniques.

ODIN'S GATEWAYS

A PRACTICAL GUIDE
TO THE WISDOM OF THE RUNES
THROUGH GALDR, SIGILS, AND CASTING

Katie Gerrard

Published by Avalonia

ACKNOWLEDGEMENTS

My first acknowledgement must be to the runes themselves for interacting with me and teaching me their lessons. My second must go to the Norse gods, and especially to Odin whose influence led to the spark that created this book. I thank those people who were a part of the course that spawned this book, and especially those who asked questions which challenged me and made me think about my own beliefs. And finally to the people who have made this book a reality, my army of proofreaders, those friends who patiently listened to my ramblings, my husband Gareth who has accompanied me throughout my journey and kept me grounded when working with the runes carried away pieces of my sanity, and Ross Brazier who aided and abetted my early experiments with the more intense runes.

Cover Art by Laura Daligan.
Find out more about Laura and her artwork by visiting:
www.lauradaligan-art.com

TABLE OF CONTENTS

Section 3
Do you know how to carve? 127

INTRODUCTION

The runes are a complex, archaic system that comprises 24 symbols each with their own voice and energy. Each rune has a different energy, strong and powerful, that has its own identity and meaning. The energy *is* the rune. It can be channelled and identified by the sigil, the name, and the sound, but the energy itself remains the core of what we are working with. The runes can be worked with individually, or they can be combined. They can be used to heal, to grow, to understand, to curse, and to protect. They can be used to explain a situation, to give us warnings, or they can be used to forecast and plan our next steps. This book aims to teach you how to write them, how to read them, how to paint them, how to carve them, how to chant them, and most importantly, how to understand them.

Odin's Gateways is the product of a ten year relationship with the runes and with the Norse gods. I have considered, established, and reconsidered my theories over these years and will probably continue to do so for many years after this book has been published. The factor that created the spark that led to this book was the decision to run a four week course teaching people how to interact with and how to work with the runes. The fears that I would struggle to fill the time with relevant information were very soon replaced by the growing realisation that ten years of study brings more material than can be covered in a four week course, and this is where the spark became a seed and this book became a seed that grew and grew.

Of course, as with the majority of my journeys, the spark that birthed the course was a gift from the god Odin; Odin the Sky Father; Odin the Traveller; and Odin who gave the runes to mankind. As someone who has spent time writing about and giving talks on the goddesses of the Norse pantheon and the mysteries and witchcraft associated with the feminine, it might come as a surprise to see that my first book has been given to me by Odin and is about the runes.

I first 'met' the runes in 1996 when I was at school. Like many teenagers I was drawn to the occult and along with other forms of divination like Tarot and playing cards, a book and some small plastic runes made their way into my possession. I used these runes a fair amount, reading them for myself and for other people, but there always seemed to be something missing. The book that came with the set, and other books I read on the runes, didn't give me the key to unlocking them and the ability to meet with and listen to them. I put them away until a year later when I first went to University and joined the University Pagan Society. There I met with people who showed me books and ideas on the runes that came from a pagan context.

Thus began the start of my relationship with the Norse gods and the intensification of my relationship with the runes. Like most relationships, at the beginning it was intense, full of new experiences and high energy, with plenty of dramatic life lessons. As the years go on this relationship has mellowed. The runes and the Norse gods form an integral part of my magical life and often my daily life too.

Odin's Gateways aims to give you the tools that you need to discover the runes for yourself and to discover for yourself the ways in which they want to work with you. There is an in-depth description of each rune, the meanings that I have attributed to it, theories other authors have come up with where relevant, how to work with that rune, and the magical uses that I have found for it. These descriptions are designed to be used as signposts - they are not definitive. Through using this book you will learn how to interact with the runes in such a way that they will teach you what they need you to know. You are likely to find your own meanings based on your own life lessons and on the stories and visions they give to you.

A note on spelling

Where using Norse and Anglo-Saxon names I have Anglicised spellings. These changes have been made in order to make the text easier to read. Where a word has more than one accepted spelling (for example Othin/Odin) I have tried to choose the most common form.

Section 1

DO YOU KNOW HOW TO ASK?

This section looks at the background information we have on the runes. It explores their possible historical use and introduces you to the way that modern rune practitioners work with them. It explores the mythology associated with the runes and the literature written about them, and offers a brief history of their transformation from an alphabet of the past to a living magical system used by a wide range of people today.

Chapter 1

LETTING THE RUNES LEAD YOU

Learning the runes is a journey. It is important to try to discover your own views and insights, rather than simply memorising the meanings that others have given them. To do this, you need to experience the individual runic energies, putting yourself on the road that allows them to teach you their individual lessons. How you learn those lessons will depend greatly on how deeply you want to get in touch with the energies. Will you learn life lessons? Will you encounter people in situations that need you to understand the runes to help them? Will you meet them in pathworkings and meditations? Will you allow them to enter your dreams? You might surprise yourself and more importantly, the runes may surprise you. Dedicating to the path of learning this knowledge should not be undertaken lightly. Are you ready for the challenge?

It is important to understand that, just like many things, the more you learn about and from the runes, the less you feel you know them. A little knowledge allows you to work with the runes and gives you the confidence to interact with the energies. When you begin to truly learn about them rune by rune you realise how little you actually know, and how much more there is to experience. Your journey might take you many years to complete. You might be like me and find that ten years later you are still studying and seeking. Hopefully, by the end of this book, you will have the tools that you need to either start or strengthen your relationship with the runes. Hopefully you will be keen to put all of this into practise and continue your study of the runes in both a practical and intuitive way.

It is difficult to teach someone the runes. Learning the runes is about experiencing them and coming to a decision about what they mean to you. Reading about the runes and the teaching of other people can give you a helping hand along the way. In the same way that I can tell you that red is a bright, primary colour, and the colour of poppies and fresh blood, I can tell you that Fehu is associated with cattle, which is in turn associated with wealth. What I can't tell you about red is the way that it makes you feel, or how warm you think it is, or what room in your house it will look good in; and I can't tell you those kinds of specifics about the runes either. I need to show you red to allow you to work out for yourself the answer to those questions. In the same way, I need to show you the runes in order for you to form an answer to your questions.

How can you show someone the runes? As we have discussed, every one of them has a different energy. These energies can be channelled by those who have worked with them. They can be channelled by calling them (intoning, chanting), or by drawing them, or by describing them. The opinions and experiences of the author can only teach you so much. By learning the voices of the runes and how to channel the energy of each one so that you can meet and experience it, you can form your own opinions and live your own experiences.

Runic alphabets are known as futharks. This is because the first letters of many of the runic alphabets spell out the word *futhark* (the Thurisaz rune is pronounced as *'th'* as we will see in more detail later). Often the first six letters of the runic alphabet are spelt in English as *futhorc*. The futhark used in this book is the Elder Futhark (see below). This is partly because it is believed that the Elder Futhark was the first set[1] but also because it is the most widely used. It is easier to work with something that other people have worked with before. This is because you are able to learn from their experience, but also because the energies themselves are fresher and more accessible *'more easily trod'*. You might find that you are happier using a different rune set at a later date, or that you learn several of them. You might even find that you decide to add a couple of the runes from the other futharks to personalise your set. It's all down to your needs.

---

1 Runes, Elliott, 1959

Chapter 2

HISTORY OF THE RUNES

The runes started out life as an early Northern European alphabet with the Elder Futhark originating in the Germanic lands. The word rune means *'mystery'* or *'hidden'*[2] and there is evidence to suggest that the runes themselves may have formed more than simply an alphabet to the Norse people. The Elder Futhark has been pieced together from sources that have suggested that it is a full alphabet divided into three distinct groups of eight (the *aetts*).

There has not been clear archaeological evidence to support where the Elder Futhark runes originated but it has been suggested that they evolved from alphabets from Northern Italy.[3] From the Elder Futhark evolved a selection of different runic alphabets. Around the 9th Century the Scandinavian countries evolved later versions of futharks which took away many of the letters (bringing the number of runes down to sixteen). These evolved further when it became clear that more letters were needed in order to represent all the sounds of the language, and dots were used within the runes in order to distinguish between different pronunciations.[4]

The names and pronunciations of the runes differ depending on what book you read and what language you are calling them in. I find that the majority channel better using the Germanic names. However, there is the odd rune that, to me, seems happier with its Anglo-Saxon name. Within this book the runes are referred to using their Germanic names, although their Anglo-Saxon names are also given. You will find, however, that when the runic voices are given, a few of these are given using their Anglo-Saxon names. You might prefer to use the names

---

2 Runes, Elliott, 1959
3 Runes, Elliott, 1959
4 Runes, Elliott, 1959

closest to your native language, or you might feel happier seeing how each rune resonates.

The Elder Futhark

Younger Futhark

Within Anglo-Saxon Britain the evolution of the runic alphabet meant that more runes were added giving us the Anglo-Saxon and the Northumbrian Rune Alphabets. [5]

Anglo-Saxon Futhark

Northumbrian Futhark

---

5 Runes, Elliott, 1959

There are a few hints within the sagas that the runes might have been more than just writing.[6] There are several instances of them being used for magical purposes. For example, in *Egil's Saga*[7] the runes appear several times described as being used supernaturally for healing, weather control, and cursing. Descriptions of the runes in the sagas show rune workers marking them in order to create a supernatural change. We can read this in one of two ways. The first is to consider it literally, that the runes themselves were used magically and therefore the power was in using the right runes for the right purposes. The second is that they were used to create incantations (Galdr) and verses that were written in runic script. This echoes the use of Latin within Medieval British folk magic.[8] Galdr is often described as being a song or an incantation so theoretically can represent any words of power used within a magical context.[9]

The runic alphabet fell out of use as Scandinavia became Christianised.[10] Runes continued to be used on gravestones after this time and also used to name things like swords and spindles[11]. The act of giving a sword a fighting name and writing it on in runic script can be seen to be a magical act in itself. Within England the Anglo-Saxon language was slowly gaining more and more Latin words and the use of the runic script gave way to the Latin alphabet. Interestingly, there are still clues to the use of runes within the English language, the most prominent example being the word '*Ye*' as in '*Ye Old Tea Shop*'. The Y is a misread of the thorn rune, which originally was depicted "Þ" but lost its ascender in Middle and Early Modern English, so that it became almost indistinguishable from the letter "Y". The thorn rune was used for the '*th*' sound, as in '*thick*', therefore '*ye old*' should read '*the old*'[12].

---

6 Runes, Elliott, 1959
7 Egil's Saga, Penguin Classics
8 Sorceress or Witch, Morris, 1991
9 See Galdrbok, Johnson & Wallis, 2005
10 Runes, Elliott, 1959
11 Rune Magic, Pennick, 1992
12 Runes, Elliott, 1959

Interestingly, runes were not given up easily by the Scandinavian people. There are accounts of people being found with them in their possession as late as the sixteenth century and a law was passed at this time forbidding the use of runes.[13] This suggests that they were considered to be more important to the Scandinavian people than being just an alphabet of antiquity, and that the magical practises of the runes in the sagas continued to be used by the Scandinavian people after they stopped being used as an alphabet. This may be a reflection of the fact that Christianity came relatively late to Scandinavia compared with mainland Europe.

THE AETTS

In the Elder Futhark, the runes are separated into three aetts, or families, comprising the eight runes within that grouping. Each aett is usually named after the first rune within the set of eight – Fehu's Aett, Hagalaz's Aett, Tiwaz's Aett. Alternatively the aetts can be linked to Norse deities; the first aett being Freyja's Aett (or Freyr's Aett),[14] the second being Hel's Aett, and the third Tyr's aett.

The first aett of the Elder Futhark is mostly associated with individuals; personal wealth, bravery, anger, wisdom, sacrifice, and joy. The second aett is associated more with the natural world; winter, spring, trees, and the sun. The third aett seems to be associated with abstract concepts; justice, motherhood, mankind, family, beginnings and endings. However, there are runes in each aett that don't fall neatly into these categories.

The positioning of the runes within the aetts is interesting as often they lead into each other, following a story. For example, the three winter runes – Hagalaz, Nauthiz, and Isa, are followed by Jera, the harvest. The positioning of these four runes within the futhark, and their interaction with each other, helps us to understand their meaning.

---

13 Runes, Elliott, 1959
14 Rune Rede, Grimnisson, 2001
14 Galdrbok, Johnson & Wallis, 2005

THE HAVAMAL

Another text that helps us glimpse the meanings of the runes is *The Havamal* which translates as *'Sayings of the High One'*[15] (the *'High One'* being the god Odin). The *Havamal* is written in 164 stanzas, of which the majority offers advice on various aspects of life in the Norse world. Towards the end of the piece, it becomes clear that the advice is being given to someone called Loddfafnir. Nathan J Johnson and Robert J Wallis[16] suggest that Loddfafnir translates as *'ragged dragon'* and can be considered a seeker or learner. They compare Loddfafnir to the Fool in the Tarot deck. Perhaps the significance of the dragon is the link to preconscious, suggesting that Loddfafnir is just learning language and the ability to interact in society. Another possible interpretation would be to link the dragon with the warrior or viking, as dragon heads were often pictured on the front and back of viking boats. Are the High One's words a code of conduct for warriors and explorers?

Certainly, the *Havamal* is written in a way that suggests that Odin is teaching the lessons of society and how to live alongside other people in harmony. The *Havamal* gives us a code of conduct and a set of ethics. Much of the information we have about Norse ethics and morality comes from the *Havamal* and shows us the importance that the Norse put in family and the ancestors. It also teaches us of the need that the Norse had to keep their loved ones alive after their death through telling stories about the past:

> *"Cattle die, Kinsmen die,*
> *The self must also die;*
> *I know one thing which never dies:*
> *The reputation of each dead man."*[17]

The *Havamal* explains about the need for exchange and for looking after other people in their times of need. Visitors are

---

15 The Poetic Edda, translation Carolyne Larrington
16 Galdrbok, Nathan & Wallis, 2005
17 The Poetic Edda, translation Carolyne Larrington

always welcomed and given the best food and chairs in the house, but visitors must pay for the hospitality they receive in gifts, or in entertaining the household with new stories (and gossip).

Many of the meanings we can glean from the runes can be referenced back to the *Havamal* to gain further insight into how those meanings might be subtly different when considered from a Norse mindset. In addition, theories on the meanings and uses for each rune can be expanded or explained by using the *Havamal* to guide us.

The final stanzas of the *Havamal* discuss how the god Odin discovered the runes. They begin by telling the story of how the runes came to Odin:

> *"I know I hung on a windy tree*
> *Nine long nights,*
> *Wounded by a spear, dedicated to Odin,*
> *Myself to myself,*
> *On that tree of which no man knows*
> *From where its roots run*
>
> *No bread did they give me nor drink from a horn,*
> *Downwards I peered;*
> *I took up the runes, screaming I took them,*
> *Then I fell back from there."*[18]

We interpret this as Odin hanging himself from the world tree Yggdrasil for nine days and nine nights without food or drink, wounded by a spear. Odin's sacrifice to Odin, the agreement that he has made with himself in order to gain the wisdom that he needs. On the final day he eventually sees and takes the runes, screaming. The next stanza talks about the runes as powerful and great letters which were stained and carved.

---

18 The Poetic Edda, translation Carolyne Larrington

"The runes you must find and the meaningful letter,
A very great letter,
A very powerful letter,
Which the mighty sage stained
And the powerful gods made
And the runemaster of the gods carved out."[19]

The *Havamal* goes on to say:

"Do you know how to carve; do you know how to interpret,
Do you know how to stain, do you know how to test out,
Do you know how to ask, do you know how to sacrifice,
Do you know how to dispatch, do you know how to slaughter?"[20]

It then goes on to discuss the spells that Odin knows and gives eighteen different stanzas detailing eighteen different spells. These are given to us almost as though they describe individual runes and the spells that they can be used for. Does this hint that the runes were used for magic in the time when the *Havamal* was written?

Another possibility is that the *Havamal* is discussing different words of power that can be used for spells or for influencing people rather than the individual runes themselves. Certainly, it isn't always clear which rune is being discussed in the *Havamal*. The Elder Futhark has 24 runes; The Old Norse Rune Poem has 16 runes. The *Havamal* discusses 18 runes. If we take the first 18 runes from the Elder Futhark and try and match them with the stanzas in the *Havamal* they don't fit, although it is possible to take certain runes out of the aetts and match them with the stanzas in a different order.

There has been some discussion on the myth of Odin's sacrifice and gain and what it really represents. It might be the step mankind made forward when he began to read and write, but it might just as easily represent the beginning of social

---

19 The Poetic Edda, translation Carolyne Larrington
20The Poetic Edda, translation Carolyne Larrington

language. There is also a school of thought that the runes were always considered to be a magical language, and therefore Odin gained the runes with all of their powers and energies. Certainly, the ability to use written words is spectacular and can be seen as magical to those who cannot. Those who could read and write were privy to more wisdom than those who could not, simply for having the ability to pass information onto each other without being in the same place.

THE RUNE POEMS

An Anglo-Saxon and an Old Norse Rune Poem exist describing each of the runes and their meaning. There is also an Icelandic Rune Poem. It is possible that instead of describing what the rune meant and how it was used the poems were originally used to describe the sound of the letters. Rather like A is for apple, B is for bear. Perhaps we are reading too much into the poems in looking to them to explain the meaning of each letter? How strange it would seem to us if someone was trying to use our language to understand the true meaning of an A symbol and its association with the apple?

R.W.V. Elliott suggests that there is more to the rune poems than simply a writing exercise.[21] He points out the richness of the symbolism included in the poetry and suggests instances where the Anglo-Saxon Rune Poem seems to be talking about folklore. Certainly, the rune poems offer an interesting insight into the societies that they have come from. Elliott[22] highlights this and discusses the importance of looking at the imagery and symbolism within the rune poems in an attempt to fully understand the culture that they came from. Considering the language and imagery within the rune poems not only helps us to understand more about the Norse society, but it also helps us to gain a deeper understanding of the energy that the runes they are describing represent.

----

21 Runes, Elliott, 1959
22 Runes, Elliott, 1959

Names and words are powerful and by linking A with Apple it means that a generation of children have grown up thinking about apples as soon as they think of the letter A. When I was at school a K was described as looking as though it was kicking and this is a vision that still comes to me when I consider the shape of the letter. Ideas and imagery can form a place in popular consciousness and therefore take their place in the collective unconscious which therefore gives the rune poems and their symbolism a greater significance than we first allotted to them.

The Old Norse Rune Poem in particular uses lines that seem to be designed as riddles. These riddles when cracked sometimes allude back to the mythology and stories of the Norse gods. As we have discussed, there is evidence to suggest that the runes were used by the Norse people within magic and spell craft for a long time after Scandinavia was Christianised. Is it too far a leap of faith to consider that the riddles within the Old Norse Rune Poem are hiding examples of how those runes can be used within a pagan context?

TACITUS

Possibly the earliest mention of *'casting'* the runes and the use of runes for divination comes from a small paragraph written by the Roman historian Tacitus.[23] Tacitus' *Germania* is an early anthropological work describing the people of Germania (the Germanic lands) and their customs. He highlighted the differences he saw between the Germanic people and his own people, the Romans. The *Germania* forms an important document for those of us wishing to study ancient Northern Europe and holds information on many aspects of life including religion. Tacitus' work also includes information on divination and magic that links to the feminine mysteries and the practise of seidr.[24]

---

23 The Germania, Tacitus, Penguin Classics
24 Seidr is the name given to the Norse Magical practise associated with witchcraft, and shamanism. See The Nine Worlds of Seid-Magic, Blain, 2001

We only have one small paragraph in Tacitus that might be describing something similar to casting runes. Although it is small, this paragraph is undeniably useful:

> "Their procedure in casting lots is always the same. They cut off a branch of a nut bearing tree and slice it into strips; these they mark with different signs and throw them completely at random onto a white cloth. Then the priest of the state, if the consultation is a public one, or the father if it is private, offers a prayer to the gods, and looking up at the sky picks up three strips, one at a time, and reads their meaning from the signs previously scored on them."[25]

This description of casting wooden lots tells us several things; the importance of a nut bearing tree and white cloth; that these signs were carved onto strips of wood; and that the meanings were interpreted in answer to a query of importance. The paragraph does not tell us if the signs marked were runes, nor does it tell us what these signs were or what they represented. Tacitus describes signs rather than words, which allows us to assume that they were symbols that he did not recognise (or did not see close up).

The image that it throws up for me, however, is one that bears a close resemblance to using wooden rune staves for casting and reading in the form of divination. The significance put onto the reading is clearly important, and Tacitus goes on to say that decisions were made based on what the interpretation of these strips was. How far is this from the way that we cast and read the runes today?

---

25 The Germania, Tacitus, Penguin Classics

Chapter 3

THE USE OF THE RUNES IN MODERN TIMES

Although runes have been studied from an academic point of view for many years, it was not until the late 20th century when the use of runes, especially the Elder Futhark, for divination really exploded. Prior to the surge in their popularity in the 1980s, significant experts and authors on the runes tended to be those who wrote about them from an academic angle (R.I. Page[26] and R.W.V. Elliott[27]). The academic and eminent scholar of the English Language J.R.R. Tolkien used the idea to make up his own alphabet.[28]

In the modern era, runes tend to be less popular than some of the better known divination tools like Tarot cards or crystal balls, but the general public is more likely to think about them in terms of divination than any of the other uses for runes. The association of runes with divination has entered popular culture and is unlikely to be shaken any time soon. In fact, the majority of books published on runes today, concentrate on their use for divination.

Perhaps the first surge of using the runes for magical purposes started with the mystic Guido Von List. Inspired by Madame Blavatsky's *Secret Doctrine*[29] and while recovering from a cataract operation he received what he referred to as '*the secret of the runes*' which he used to develop a system of using the runes for magic.[30] Based on the information given in the *Havamal*, he created a new set of runes that he called Armanen which contained eighteen runes, the same number as stanzas within the *Havamal*. Guido Von List's study of the runes became part of occultism within Nazi German thinking. This association with Nazi Germany and the further link that people

---

26 Runes and Runic Inscriptions, Page, first essay date 1958
27 Runes: An Introduction, Elliott, 1959
28 The Lord of the Rings, Tolkien, 1954
29 Science of the Swastika, Mees, 2008
30 Futhark, Thorsson, 1984

sometimes draw towards white supremacy occasionally puts people off of working with the runes. It is important to remember that the runes were around long before Nazi occultism borrowed the concepts. The strength of the runes is greater than any residue of misuse and, in my experience; the runes remain untainted by their association.

There are two names that you will find associated time and time again with the birth of rune use in the modern era; Ralph Blum, who published *The Book of Runes* in 1984[31] and Edred Thorsson (also known as Stephen Flowers) who published *Futhark: A Handbook of Rune Magic* in 1984.[32] Before these two authors, books on the runes tended to be more academic and less practical. The modern use of the runes as a divination tool was something that very little was heard about before this time.

Blum was the first person to popularise runes in the mainstream and make them a part of the New Age movement. Blum is thought to have been the originator of the blank rune[33] a subject on which there is a detailed discussion in the sub-section below this one. An internet search or a discussion with those who work with runes tells you very quickly that there are some very strong opinions regarding the blank rune. Sweyn Plowright tells us that there is a divide between traditionalists who *'fume'* at the mention of the blank rune and New Agers who love it.[34] Many in the heathen community have reacted negatively towards Blum's interpretation of the runes.

The order of the runes is different in Blum's books to the traditional order of the Elder Futhark. Does this invalidate the information that he gives about each rune? When we consider this we need to consider the vast number of futharks found by archaeologists all containing slightly different runes in slightly different orders. We also need to remember that the placing of the final two runes, Othala and Dagaz are often switched.

If you have read any book that mentions the blank rune, bought a set of runes that come with an instruction book, or

---

31 The Book of Runes, Blum, 1984
32 Futhark, Thorsson, 1984
33 A Down to Earth Guide to the Runes, Plowright, 2007
34 A Down to Earth Guide to the Runes, Plowright, 2007

bought any kind of rune cards or plastic runes, then it is likely that they were either by Ralph Blum or by someone who has been heavily influenced by him.

Thorsson came to the runes from a different angle to Blum. Thorsson wanted to study, recreate, and ritualise the Old Norse religion and practises, and founded the Rune Guild and the Ring of Troth. He used runes for galdr and within rituals[35] as well as for divination and heavily relied on the information given within the rune poems for his work. He had also read and been influenced by the work of Guido Von List.[36] In Thorsson's book *Futhark*[37] there is no blank rune and each rune is looked at within the context of Norse mythology and society. Thorsson tackles the subject of the runes from a mindset and viewpoint that is deliberately Norse and it is clear that he has a relationship with the runes and the Norse gods throughout his writing.

Following on from Thorsson were Freya Aswynn[38] and Jan Fries[39]. These authors also came to the runes from an occult context and their relationship with the runes also incorporated a relationship with the Norse gods. Although there have been other authors writing on the runes, I consider these two authors, out of the collection of authors whose work followed 1984, to have made the largest impact on modern rune practise. Freya Aswynn's work is so influential because she expresses the importance of really getting in touch with the runes and living them. Aswynn worked with each individual rune, learning its lessons, feeling its energy, meditating on the rune, reading the primary sources, and intoning and chanting their names. Aswynn would take each rune into herself by eating it drawn onto a cake in order to fully assimilate its energy and live with it.[40]

---

35 Galdrabok, Flowers, 1989
36 Futhark, Thorsson, 1984
37 Futhark, Thorsson, 1984
38 Leaves of Yggdrasil, Aswynn, 1988
39 Helrunar, Fries, 1993
40 Leaves of Yggdrasil, Aswynn, 1988

Jan Fries took this formula onwards and added to it his experience within ritual magic as well as his research on the magical artist Austin Osman Spare.[41] Fries also took and developed Thorsson's hand gestures and body postures that he used to channel the runes and harness their energy. Fries work within this area remains some of the most comprehensive.

THE BLANK RUNE

There has been much debate about the blank rune. The idea seems to have originated with Ralph Blum who got the idea from a set of handmade runes he bought in the 1970s.[42] Blum describes it as *'wyrd'* or *'fate'*. He also refers to it as Odin's Rune.[43]

One of the *'urban myths'* concerning the origin of the blank rune is that Ralph Blum's runes (that came free with the book) were easier to manufacture on a five tiles by five stamp than in a six tiles by four or an eight tiles by three matrix and therefore it was simply more work to take the blank rune out than to keep it in.[44] I have not been able to find the source of this theory, although it has become more widely repeated in pagan circles in the last five years.

In Norse mythology, fate can be seen as being represented by the web of wyrd, which is woven by the Norns (goddesses who are similar to the Greco-Roman three Fates) who in doing so are weaving the fates of mankind. The Norns are sometimes said to write fate, however, the goddess Frigga is said to spin the thread that is woven by the Norns into wyrd.[45] Frigga is said to be able to see what is going to happen but not to be able to initiate changes in what must be. Therefore, the question is who is responsible for writing the fate of mankind (if anyone or

---

41 The Writings of Austin Osman Spare, published in 2007 is probably the best book to learn more about Spare. Visual Magick, 1992 shows Fries work with Spare's teachings in more detail.
42 A Down to Earth Guide to the Runes, Plowright, 2007
43 Book of Runes, Blum, 1984
44 Rig Svenson, http://www.pendamoot.co.uk/blankrune.html
45 Edda, Snorri Sturluson, Everyman

anything)? Is it the thread itself? Or Frigga? Or the Norns? Or is it simply that fate exists and will follow its path whatever actions are taken with it?

The blank rune therefore represents that which is unknown or not able to be seen, a sort of metaphoric shrug. Those I have met who use the blank rune say that they do so because they like to have a response for *'I don't know'* or *'hidden'*. Some people have likened it to the Tarot card *'The Wheel of Fortune'* and take its meaning from that which is commonly ascribed to this Tarot card. There are runes that hold similar meanings, Pertho can represent fate, and the Ansuz rune can easily be described as *'Odin's rune'*.

Personally, I do not use the blank rune. There are a few reasons why this is and the first is because when I cast the runes for divination I do so using the whole set. I do this by throwing the runes onto a surface and looking at the way in which they interact with each other. This gives the opportunity for 24 runes to remain *'hidden'* and *'blank'* if they wish to. The second reason is because I choose to use the Elder Futhark of 24 runes in three sets of eight. To add an extra rune unbalances this and I can't see which aett the blank rune would fit into. Perhaps the most important reason for me choosing to not use the blank rune is because it is impossible for me to work with the shape of the rune, or the sound, when it has neither. A blank rune is shapeless which by rights should also mean that it also has no voice. If I want to chant the rune's name, do I chant *'blank'* or *'fate'*? I learn about the runes through their voice and a rune that has no shape and no voice therefore becomes unreachable. It becomes like air or like the colours of light that I cannot see. I might be able to believe that it exists or to see the effects of it but I cannot interact with it, or paint with it, or give it form and shape.

Whether or not you choose to use the blank rune is something that must be personal to your working. If you choose to use the blank rune do so because you feel that it adds value to your working and you can find a use for it in all aspects of your runic work, not just within divination. If you choose not to use the blank rune do so not just because it is a recent invention (to do so is to ignore something because it is not the 'right' way of doing things – is there any 'right' way with something as old as the runes?) but because you feel that it does not add anything to your rune work.

Chapter 4

THE NINE WORLDS

Understanding the runes is also about looking into the core of what they represent. Part of doing this has to be exploring Germanic and Norse society and mythology. Gaining an understanding into the cosmology and beliefs of the people who used the runes throughout history is invaluable.

According to Norse mythology, the world was created from fire and ice, the two elements that form the basis of the Scandinavian landscape. The *Poetic Edda* mentions nine worlds that surround Yggdrasil, the world tree, which forms the backbone of the universe, with the nine worlds forming parts of its roots and branches:

> *"I born of giants, remember very early*
> *Those who nurtured me then;*
> *I remember nine worlds, I remember nine giant women,*
> *The mighty Measuring Tree down below the earth."*[46]

In modern times, there have been various discussions on the nine worlds and more specifically, which worlds are included and which are not. It is a common misconception that the ancient literature specifically lists what these nine worlds are. Robert J Wallis and Nathan Johnson[47] point out that sometimes the Norse worlds are discussed as numbering seven. In regards to this they suggest that perhaps it would make sense to number the worlds as eight which then puts them at the same number of legs as on Odin's horse Sleipnir. In my description of the nine worlds I have joined the lands of the elves (Svartalfheim and Alfheim) together, although other authors list them as separate places, as described in the *Poetic Edda*.[48] I have also

---

46 The Poetic Edda, translation Carolyne Larrington
47 Galdrbok, Johnson & Wallis, 2006
48 The Poetic Edda, translation Carolyne Larrington

listed Asgard and Vanaheim as separate, whereas some other authors combine the two realms of the gods, or leave out the world of the Vanir completely.

MIDGARD

Midgard sits in the middle of Yggdrasil. Midgard can be loosely translated as *'middle land'* or *'middle earth'* and it is often suggested that J.R.R. Tolkien borrowed the term for his book *The Lord of the Rings*.[49] Midgard is our world; the world where humans reside.

ASGARD

Asgard is at the top of the tree and this is where the race of gods and goddesses known as the Aesir live. Asgard can be reached from Midgard by a rainbow bridge known as Bifrost. The Chief of the Aesir is the god Odin who is married to the goddess Frigga. Odin has two brothers Villi and Ve, and he has two sons (with Frigga) Baldur and Hod. Odin is the god of wisdom and also of warriors and battle. Odin's hall Valhalla is where half of the warriors who died with a sword in their hand are said to reside after death. Frigga can be described as the goddess of fate and is also connected with wisdom (perhaps more suitably described as cunning). Other members of the Aesir include Tyr, the god of sacrifice and justice; Idunna, who provides the apples of youth; Thor, the god of travelling and thunder (and was perhaps the most widely worshipped among the Norse people);[50] Thor's wife Sif, the goddess of the corn; and Heimdall, who guards the entrance of Asgard. There are others who live in Asgard, notably the fire entity Loki who is Odin's blood brother and long-term guest, as well as Freyja, Freyr, and Njord of the Vanir.

---

49 The Lord of the Rings, Tolkien, 1954
50 Gods and Myths of Northern Europe, Davidson, 1973

VANAHEIM

Vanaheim is often depicted at the top of Yggdrasil along with Asgard, and is where the race of gods known as the Vanir lives. According to Norse mythology, the gods in Asgard and Vanaheim were at war for many years. This war ended when two hostages were exchanged. The Aesir hostage didn't fare so well but Njord, the Vanir hostage went on to live in Asgard and was joined by his children, the twin gods Freyr and Freyja. Folklorists[51] have suggested that whereas the Aesir are connected with the development of civilisation and represent more recent religious practices, the Vanir were the original gods of the land who were connected with fertility and nature.

Of the Vanir, those who are said to live in Asgard - Njord, Freyr, and Freyja – form an intrinsic part of the myths told about the Aesir. Njord is the benevolent god of the sea-shore who calms the tempests sent by Aegir, the more capricious god of the deep sea. Freyr is the god of fertility and the harvest, and his twin sister Freyja is the goddess of sexuality and witchcraft. Freyja has first choice of the battle-slain warriors for her hall in Asgard, Sessrumnir.[52] It is also said that this is where women who commit suicide live after death.[53] Britt Mari Nasstrom[54] expands on this by explaining that women who suffer a noble death (however that may be) are the ones that live in Sessrumnir after their death.

JOTUNHEIM

Jotunheim is the hall of the giants. The Norse myths include many stories about giants.[55] The creation myth tells us that giants came into being before the gods and before mankind. The giants were often depicted as the enemies of the gods, and can be seen to represent the forces of chaos, whereas the gods

51 Gods and Myths of Northern Europe, Davidson, 1973
52 Edda, Snorri Sturluson, Everyman
53 Egil's Saga, Penguin translation
54 Freyja, Great Goddess of the North, Nasstrom, 1995
55 The Penguin Book of Norse Myths, Holland, 1996

represent the forces of order. Thor especially is involved in many stories where he has to compete with the giants both with his strength and his wit. Thor's hammer Mjollnir was created in order to protect Asgard from the giants. However, it should be noted that both Odin and Thor were said to have been descended from the giants.[56]

ALFHEIM/ LJOSALFHEIM/ SVARTALFHEIM

Alfheim is where the elves live. Ancient Norse literature describes the elves as beautiful, and in some cases as the ghosts of the dead, who watch over the living. In many ways they can be seen as akin to fairies. The god Freyr is said to be the Lord of the Elves, and it may be the elves represent lesser gods and spirits of the natural world. In the *Poetic Edda*, the elves are divided into the light elves who live in Ljosalfheim and the dark elves (or black elves) who live in Svartalfheim and are identical to the dwarves.[57]

NIDAVELLIR

Nidavellir is the hall of the dwarves. The dwarves are described as a race of beings that are smaller in stature than the gods. Their appearance is looked upon unfavourably in the myths (for example, Freyja was taunted by Loki[58] for having had sex with dwarves) but their craftsmanship was admired. In more than one myth the gods go to the dwarves to create something that they need. Mjollnir, Thor's hammer and Brisingamen, Freyja's necklace were both created by the dwarves.

---

56 Edda, Snorri Sturluson, Everyman
57 Heimskringla, Snorri Sturluson
58 The Poetic Edda, translation Carolyne Larrington (Lokasenna)

MUSPELLHEIM

Muspellheim is the place of primal fire, and home to the fire giants ruled by Surtr. It is Muspellheim, the fiery world at the bottom of Yggdrasil, rather than cold and dark Helheim that seems to fit the image of the Christian Hell from Dante's *Divine Comedy*.

NIFLHEIM

Niflheim is the land of the cold mists. Muspellheim and Niflheim are at the base of Yggdrasil, just above Helheim. According to Norse mythology, it was the combined energies of the fires of Muspellheim and ice of Niflheim that first gave form to the great void from which all creation sprang.

HELHEIM/ NIFLHEL/ HEL

Helheim is the hall of the dead that forms the roots of Yggdrasil. Unlike the Christian idea of Hell, the Norse did not see Helheim as a place of punishment for the dead; simply the place where those who died of natural causes (old age or sickness) resided after their death. The majority of Norse people would expect to live in Helheim after their death. Those who were lucky or ambitious might hope to spend their afterlife in one of the halls of the gods, but the majority would make the journey to Helheim.

Helheim was ruled over by the goddess Hel who was half alive and half dead; half fresh and young, and half rotten. Hel was one of Loki's children by the giantess Angrboda, and was sent to rule over Helheim by the Aesir.[59] Hel's role in the myths is interesting, as her job looking after Helheim is an important one, and she is generally seen here in a positive light.

---

59 The Penguin Book of Norse Myths, Holland, 1996

PRIMARY AND SECONDARY SOURCES :
GERMANIC AND NORSE MYTHOLOGY

Much of the information we have on Norse beliefs and culture comes from the collection of ancient Icelandic stories often referred to as *'the Sagas'*, these are available in various translations and include the *Saga of Eirik the Red*, *Egil's Saga*, *Laxdaela Saga*, *Orkneyinga Saga*, *Njal's Saga*, and *King Harald's Saga*. There are other collections of stories you can look at such as the Seven Viking Romances.

The most widely read primary source on Norse mythology is Snorri Sturluson's *Edda* (also known as the *Prose Edda* or *Younger Edda*).[60] However, Snorri Sturluson was a Christian writing about 1200, and so it is unclear how much he may have been influenced by Christian ideas and mythology. The *Poetic Edda* is a collection of Norse poems, contained within the Codex Regis manuscript, written in 13th century Iceland.[61] Although the *Poetic Edda* was written around the same time as Snorri's *Edda*, the *Poetic Edda* is considered to be compiled from older traditional sources, hence its alternative name of the *Elder Edda*. The *Poetic Edda* is a rich source for anyone interested in Norse magical practices and the runes, and includes the *Havamal* and some interesting sources for the study of seidr (for example the poem *Voluspa*). In addition to the Eddas, much information on Germanic beliefs and practices can be found in early Anglo-Saxon sources such as *Beowulf*[62] or the *Battle of Maldon*.[63]

Secondary sources on Germanic and Norse beliefs tend to be written by historians and folklorists who have studied the primary sources from an academic point of view. Although these types of books can appear to be very dry, they are invaluable to anyone seeking to understand more about the runes and the culture they sprang from. Authors to look out for include H.R.

---

60 Edda, Snorri Sturluson, Everyman
61 The Poetic Edda, translation Carolyne Larrington, Oxford World Classics
62 Beowulf, Penguin Classics
63 Battle of Maldon, translation, Bill Griffiths

Ellis Davidson, Tony Linsell, and Brian Branston. In addition there is a wealth of information available from modern authors on the use of runes. Some of the better books are by practising pagan authors who live and breathe the runes in their daily lives, and who have a deep understanding of the use of the runes. These authors include Freya Aswynn, Jan Fries, and Diana Paxson.

Section 2

Do you know how to interpret?

This section introduces you to the runes. It looks at how to channel them and experience their energy, and how to use the rune poems and the shape and voice to learn more about their meanings.

Before you start working with the runes, find yourself a notebook or binder specifically to write down and keep all the information you learn about each individual rune. A binder means that you can add more and more pages as you go along, but notebooks are often smaller and easier to carry around. You may find it convenient to divide your note book into enough sections for each rune before you start, so that you can refer back to them quickly and easily.

Note down the experiences you have in conjunction with each rune, as well as any visions and insights you get from meeting it. You should also make a note of any new ideas that come to you when you are reading for other people. Finally, write in anything that you have read or heard from other rune workers. Note down who said what to make it easier to refer back to later.

Chapter 5

MEETING ODIN

Even if you are not a practising Pagan, or if you don't believe in the existence of the Norse gods, it is still a good idea to get in tune with the *'Odinic energy'* before you embark on any serious work with the runes. According to Norse mythology, the runes were given to mankind by Odin[64] who the *Havamal* tells us gained them through his sacrifice to himself by hanging on Yggdrasil for nine days with no food or drink. If you are working with the runes or have decided to work with the runes, there is a good chance that you are working with Odin and the Norse gods in some way already. If you are not, then your experiences with the runes will be greatly enhanced by getting to know Odin and the Norse gods.

By working with the runes you are working within a magical system that is intrinsically linked to Odin. The Ansuz rune in particular is intimately associated with Odinic energy; many of the other runes contain symbolism that also links directly back to him. Starting your journey with the runes by connecting to Odin allows you to put yourself in touch with the primordial energy that the runes came from, and gives you the chance to gain any advice or wisdom that he wishes to impart to you that may help you on your way.

Part of asking for Odin's guidance requires an exchange. What do you give to Odin, or what will you do for Odin in order to gain the wisdom of the runes? By asking for help from Odin without offering him something in return, we run the risk of having something taken from us that we might not have originally offered. The *Havamal* teaches us about the importance of an exchange[65] and you will find the wisdom gained from this exchange all the more precious for it. Your gift to Odin need not be as dramatic as his own sacrifice to himself;

---

64 The Havamal, The Poetic Edda, Everyman translation
65 The Poetic Edda, translation Carolyne Larrington

a poem, sketch or other creative work dedicated to Odin, or an agreement to spend a certain amount of time working with the runes would be fine. Alternatively you might want to make a donation to a charity associated with Odin's animals – wolves and ravens.

JOURNEYING TO MEET WITH ODIN

Going on a pathworking meditation (also known as journeying) to meet with Odin is a great way to make contact with him. A pathworking is basically a structured meditation during which you follow a predetermined path or journey.[66] It is important to have a clear intent or task for any pathworking, and it is advisable to set yourself a time limit before you start. For this journey the task is to *'journey to Asgard to meet with Odin and gain advice on how to work with the runes'*. Set your time limit to how experienced you are with meditating (or how in practice you are). Fifteen to twenty minutes is a good amount of time but an experienced person might want to spend longer talking to Odin, and a person with less experience might want to keep the journey to ten minutes in order to make sure that they can keep their concentration throughout the pathworking.[67]

Before you attempt the pathworking, turn off your telephone and any other potential outside distractions, and familiarise yourself with the steps of the journey, so that your subconscious can follow these steps without becoming distracted. Many people like to use drumming when journeying to help focus the active part of the mind, while allowing the subconscious to wander. More information about this useful technique can be found in *The Way of the Shaman*, by Michael Harner.[68] The Harner Method uses a rhythm of around four beats per second when journeying, and then alters the rhythm to signal to the subconscious when the time comes for you to return from the journey. This *'stop and pay attention'* signal is usually slower

---

66 For more information on pathworking see Magick Without Peers, Rainbird & Rankine, 1997
67 Another great source for journeying is Diana Paxson, Trance-portation, 2008
68 The Way of the Shaman, Harner, 1992

than the journeying rhythm, and only needs to last for a few seconds. A third, faster rhythm of around eight beats per second is used to bring the subconscious back to the mundane world. When you return from your journey, you should retrace the steps that you took on the way there (albeit significantly faster), so that your subconscious and conscious minds are properly reintegrated. Coming out of the trance state of a pathworking too quickly can be harmful. You should always ground yourself after journeying, and the easiest way to do this is to have something to eat and drink. It is also a good idea to write down your experiences straight away, as like dreams, they can often fade over time.

To begin your journey to meet Odin, find a comfortable position, close your eyes and spend a few minutes listening to your breathing and relaxing. Visualise the space you are in, and in your mind's eye, picture yourself sitting or laying in whatever position you are in. Once you are completely relaxed, imagine a white mist starting to come into the room, spiralling in from the corners and slowly getting thicker and thicker. Imagine the mist keeps coming in until it has totally clouded the view of the space you are in, and you are sitting supported by and surrounded by the mist. Visualise the mist changing colour to one that makes you feel happy and secure, and then see the mist clearing until you find yourself sitting in a place where you feel comfortable and safe. An outside space is helpful and it doesn't need to be an actual place; you can visualise a clearing in a forest or a park.

When you can clearly see your space in your mind's eye, visualise a tall, wide tree. This is Yggdrasil, the world tree that connects the nine worlds of Norse mythology. Yggdrasil is usually described as a tall Ash tree (although some people see it as a Yew tree) standing so high that you can't see the top. Visualise yourself climbing the tree, either by climbing the branches, or by seeing a doorway in the trunk open onto a stairway or a lift that takes you right to the top. At the top of the tree you see a rainbow-coloured bridge, Bifrost, and standing between you and the bridge you see the god Heimdall, a tall fair man, who carries a horn. He challenges you and you tell him why you want to go to Asgard. He lets you pass. You cross the bridge and find yourself in Asgard, home of the Aesir.

My journeying experiences within Asgard usually involve me sitting at the head of a long table in a great hall, sharing food with the various deities that have gathered there. You might see Asgard differently. At this point of the pathworking you will probably find that you don't need to work so hard at visualising, and that the pictures just come to you. Odin will be there. Usually he appears to me as a tall, beardless man with a large hat covering one eye. He wears a cloak fastened with a round brooch and has his ravens Hugin and Munin on each shoulder. He might appear differently to you, or you might see him as a person-shaped collection of energy, or as a shadow. How Odin appears is as much to do with the way in which our subconscious is able to perceive him as it is to do with the way in which he wishes to appear to us. Explain why you have journeyed to Asgard and what you wish to know. You should also agree with Odin what you will give in exchange for this knowledge.

When your time with Odin is finished (if you have set yourself a time limit you should have a sense of when it is time), thank him for meeting with you, and begin your journey back to the mundane world. This is the point, if you have chosen to drum, to give yourself the slow 'stop and pay attention' signal, followed by the faster 'come back now' rhythm. Continue drumming the 'come back now' rhythm as you return over Bifrost and make your way down Yggdrasil back into your safe space. See the coloured mist starting to come in and visualise it changing back to a white mist. As you see the white mist clearing, once more picture yourself sitting or lying in the room where you are. Take three deep breaths, stop drumming if you have used a drum, and when you feel ready, open your eyes.

Chapter 6

MEETING THE RUNES

Each rune can be considered to have its own individual energy. This energy can be harnessed and channelled in several ways; drawing its shape, meditating upon it, intoning or chanting the voice, or even adopting body postures in the shape of the rune. Different people will find different methods to be more or less potent ways to channel energy, depending on the type of person they are. I personally find that intoning the runes is a particularly powerful way to get in touch with them. By intoning and chanting the voice, we create a gateway within ourselves that allows us to channel the energy into the space we are in. We can then fully experience the energy of the rune, and harness it for use within galdr.

Take a deep breath and let it out slowly as you chant the rune. The trick is to vibrate and intone the sound rather than just calling it by name (more details on intoning can be found in the sections on the individual runes). Each rune will vibrate and resonate at a different frequency and therefore will have a different 'voice'. Focus on becoming a channel for the rune. You will feel the different voices within different parts of your body as you chant. It is easy to confuse energy with loudness. You want high levels of energy, not necessarily high levels of noise (although, as we will see later, some runes like to be shouted).

Practice controlling your breath and throwing your voice so that the energy and sound travels into the centre of the space you are working in. Visualise the energy of the rune channelling itself through you. While you are using the voice, also use the shape and sigil of the rune. You can either visualise it in front of you, lit up with light or flames and being energised by the voice, or you can trace the shape of the rune in the air, seeing it light up as you trace its shape and chant its voice.

As well as each rune having a different vibration, the voice will have its own individual pitch and sound. Each rune also has a different rhythm with emphasis on a certain syllable. To find the rune's voice, try intoning the name in different pitches and rhythm combinations until you find the one that feels right. Experiment with the names in the different languages too. You will know when you have hit upon the right voice because the energy of the rune will be obvious to you and you will notice the change in the atmosphere. You might find that several different voices will help you to channel the rune, but you should notice a distinct difference in the intensity of the energy when you have hit upon the rune's voice.

Use this shift in energy and atmospheric change to help you understand the subtle nature of the rune and its meaning. Does it bring out any particular emotion in you? Does it feel hot or cold? Does the air feel clear or heavy? You might find that the rune draws certain memories from you or that you can visualise pictures and imagery that help to explain its meaning. The sensations and feelings you gain from meeting the rune will form the basis of your understanding of it. Meeting the rune gives you the flavour of its energy.

Once you have met and experienced the rune, you can try and locate a deeper understanding of its meaning and what it can be used for. The second stage of understanding the rune comes from its sigil. Think about what the shape reminds you of. It might not be anything archaic or Norse inspired; it might be something from your modern life. You are using the runes within a modern context; therefore, all of your experiences are valid. Think of it like the inkblot test in that what you see will be coming as much from your subconscious as from the original shape the rune was designed as.

The next stage to learning and understanding the runes is to look at the rune poems. The two that I choose to work with are the Anglo-Saxon Rune Poem and the Old Norse Rune Poem. You could also use the Icelandic Rune Poem, or the *Havamal*. It is important to remember when we look at the rune poems that the runes mentioned in them may be different to those in the Elder Futhark or in a slightly different order. For example, there are only sixteen runes in the Old Norse Rune Poem, which means that at best, we can only use it to understand sixteen of the 24 runes in the Elder Futhark. Many of the later

Scandinavian futharks do have sixteen runes. The Anglo-Saxon Rune Poem does not include as many runes as are in the Anglo-Saxon Futhark (there are an additional four).

You might find that the different rune poems give different meanings to the runes. You might find that you don't understand the correlation between what you picked up when you experienced the voice of the rune, and what the rune poems say about that particular rune. The important thing here is how the rune feels to you. Often, the link between your own feelings and what the different rune poems say becomes clear once you do more research into ancient Germanic and Norse culture and mythology. Understanding more about ancient Germanic and Norse culture can help put the rune poems into context. It is also a good idea to look at the descriptions and meanings that other people use (see my own interpretations for each rune later in this chapter). All of this information together will help you to formulate your own ideas and theories. Interestingly, even if you end up disagreeing with something, in order to disagree you need to think about how someone came up with a different conclusion to you, which gives you a greater understanding yourself.

Finally, channel the rune again. You will find that your greater understanding of the rune helps you to get in touch with it more deeply, and channel it its energy more intensely through you. Intone the rune while drawing it in the air with your hand. You can either do this three times and then drum or clap to focus your mind or you can keep intoning the rune. You may find yourself entering a light trance state. Use this energy to visualise pictures as before. Let the rune 'speak' to you and you should get some ideas that further explain the meaning of the rune or how you can use it in galdr.

For an even deeper understanding of the rune, you can use it as a gateway for a pathworking. Journeying into the rune itself allows you to go and meet the rune rather than call the rune to meet you. This method of experiencing the energy of the runes is best done in addition to the voice work described above. Even if you find meditation easier than the voice work, intoning and chanting is an integral part of experiencing the rune, and will greatly empower your runic practice.

JOURNEY THROUGH THE GATEWAY OF THE RUNE

If you have limited experience with pathworkings, go back and read the guidance given in the section on journeying to meet Odin. Before you start this pathworking, state your intent and set a time limit. For journeying to meet a rune, a good intent to use is *"I am going to meet with* (state which rune you are going to meet) *and learn more about its meaning/ use."* Decide whether you want to use a drum, as described in the journey to meet Odin. If you decide not to use a drum but still want to focus your mind, you could chant the rune as you journey.

Find a comfortable position, close your eyes and spend a few minutes listening to your breathing and relaxing. Visualise yourself and the space you are in. In your mind's eye, see a white mist starting to come into the room, spiralling in from the corners and slowly getting thicker and thicker. Imagine the mist keeps coming in until it has totally clouded the view of the space you are in, and you are sitting supported by and surrounded by the mist. Visualise the mist changing colour to one that makes you feel happy and secure. While you are still surrounded by the mist, visualise yourself making the sign of the rune you are going to meet with in the air in front of you. Hear the rune's voice, and see the rune getting bigger and bigger until it becomes a gateway that you can step into. Step into the rune.[69] This is the gateway that will take you where you need to go in order to learn more about it.

Depending on what previous experience you have of pathworking you might find that it takes a bit of practise to be able to fully visualise and experience when journeying. You might find that you experience in sounds and feelings rather than in sight. You might also find that you experience in smell

---

69 Trance-Portation, Paxson, 2008 also gives information on using symbols as gateways

and touch. A journey is not just about seeing, it is about experiencing. It is good practise to try and focus the senses that don't seem to come naturally to you when visualising.

When journeying into the gateway of a rune it is important to remember that there is no one way that you will receive the information you are seeking. Sometimes you will be given pieces of information (for example words or images). Sometimes you will be given feelings and emotions associated with that rune. There will be times when your journey is clear and expressive but there may also be times when you feel that what you have experienced needs further work in order to interpret or it might be in code. The rune may also show you memories so that you can understand it through experiences you have already had.

If you have not done a lot of pathworking before and you want to undertake journeys to understand each of the runes it is worth practising and getting used to being on the astral before you start. Diana Paxson's *Trance-portation*[70] is a good book for getting you used to journeying. One concept that it is important for me to give you before you start journeying into the runes is what you need to do if you meet anything that challenges you or makes you feel unsafe.

First of all, if you have a guide, ask them to accompany you on your journeys. If you have not worked with an animal or spirit guide, why not start with a pathworking to find your guide?[71] The first thing to remember is that sometimes things appear to be something that they aren't. If you are unsure (or just as a matter of course) it is worth challenging any entities that you meet. One way of doing this is to simply demand that it show you its true identity. This often is enough for you to understand that a challenging entity is actually a concept or a part of your mind that you, having given a name and form to, are able to understand and move on from. If this concept is one that you know you need more work on but don't have time now, give it a time and a place that you will revisit (but make sure

---

70 Trance-Portation, Paxson, 2008.
71 Trance-Portation, Paxson, 2008 and The Way of the Shaman, Harner, 1982 both give very good examples of this

that you keep your promise and get any emotional help that you need beforehand).

If the challenging entity is exactly that, a challenging entity that has no place in your journey at this time, you can either banish it, or give it a time that you will dedicate to working with it (again, making sure that you get the right support before you undertake and making sure you keep your promise). If you have chosen to banish, do so firmly. *'I do not wish to encounter you on my journey so please leave me be'.* Most things will respect this. If it does not go then you need to use a bit more force. This is the time to use the Thurisaz rune and possibly the Eihwaz rune in order to call support to you (or something else that will banish for you). It is very rare that you would need to use these runes within a journey, but it is important that you are prepared should you need to.

When you are ready to come back, thank any helpers you have met, and thank the rune itself. If you are using a drum, you can use the *'stop and pay attention'* signal followed by the *'return now'* signal. Step back through the rune gateway and sit down in the mist with the rune facing you. Visualise the rune getting smaller and smaller until it disappears, then see the mist change colour back to white. Feel that you are supported by the mist and then watch it slowly begin to clear. As it clears, visualise yourself back in the space that you started from and feel yourself back in your body. Take three deep breaths and when you feel ready, open your eyes.

Chapter 7

THE RUNES

SIGIL	GERMANIC	ANGLO-SAXON	OLD NORSE	BRIEF DESCRIPTION
ᚠ	Fehu	Feoh	Fe	Cattle, wealth, currency
ᚢ	Uruz	Ur	Ur	Aurochs, strength, endurance, courage
ᚦ	Thurisaz	Thorn	Thurs	Thor's hammer, thorn, defence as attack
ᚨ	Ansuz	Os	Oss	God, Odin, voice, mouth, communication
ᚱ	Raido	Rad	Reid	Journey, astral travelling
ᚲ	Kenaz	Cen	Kaun	Torch, fire, light
ᚷ	Gebo	Gifu	None	A gift, an exchange, a sacrifice, payment
ᚹ	Wunjo	Wynn	Wenne	Joy, contentment, sexual togetherness and satisfaction, romantic partnership
ᚺ	Hagalaz	Haegl	Hagall	Hail, winter
ᚾ	Nauthiz	Nyd	Naudr	Need, hunger, want
ᛁ	Isa	Is	Is	Ice, frozen, standstill

ᛃ	Jera	Ger	Ar	Fertility, spring, corn, harvest, time
ᛇ	Eihwaz	Eoh	None	Yew, help, the crossbow
ᛈ	Pertho	Peorth	None	Fate, birth, the womb
ᛉ	Algiz/ Elhaz	Eolh	Yr	Marsh, protection, safety, warning
ᛋ	Sowilo	Sigel	Sol	The sun, warmth, healing
ᛏ	Tiwaz	Tyr	Tyr	The god Tyr, justice, sacrifice
ᛒ	Berkana	Beorc	Bjarkan	Birch, calming, healing, birth
ᛖ	Ehwaz	Eh	None	Horse, witchcraft, spaecraft, riding
ᛗ	Mannaz	Man	Madr	Mankind, partnership
ᛚ	Laguz	Lagu	Logr	Lake, water, purification, cleansing
ᛝ	Inguz	Ing	None	Sex, fertility, conception, genitals
ᛟ	Othala	Ethel	None	Ancestry, inheritance, homestead
ᛞ	Dagaz	Daeg	None	Dawn, conclusion, beginning

FEHU – FEOH - FE

"Wealth is a comfort to all men
Though each must share it well
If he will cast his 'lot' before his drihten."[72]
Anglo-Saxon Rune Poem

"(Wealth) is a source of discord among kinsmen
The wolf lives in the forest."[73]
Old Norse Rune Poem

The modern meaning for this is often given as *'cattle'* which is then translated as being *'wealth'*, or movable or transient wealth, because a person would not know how rich his cattle crop would be from year to year. One year's cattle may be good, but what of the next year?

Freya Aswynn[74] links Fehu with the word *'fee'* recognising that cattle were used as currency. The Anglo-Saxon and Old Norse Rune Poems give the meaning of Fehu as wealth, but when considering Fehu and its energy, we need to look beyond the simplicity of rich and poor.

A healthy year of calf births for a farmstead starts the year off with hope. However, the amount of calves born will depend, amongst other things, on the amount born the previous year. Also, a large amount of cows born at the start of the year doesn't guarantee a large number of cows to sell at the end of the year. Sickness, famine or even bad weather can all affect the herd,

---

72 Galdrbok, Johnson & Wallis, 2005
73 Helrunar, Fries, 1993
74 Freya Aswynn, Leaves of Yggdrasil

and therefore what the farm can sell at harvest. Therefore the hopes and fears for the wealth of Fehu rise and fall throughout the year.

If we want to draw comparisons with wealth and currency we can look at the way that the stock exchange rises and falls throughout the year. The size of the investment gives a clue as to the end amount. However, highs and lows mean that it is difficult to predict the size of the fund at the end. Currency similarly is measured in terms of how much it is worth against other currencies. Is your Fehu worth as much this year as it was last year?

The Anglo-Saxon Rune Poem talks about wealth being a comfort,[75] but that it must be bestowed freely. The Christian influence on the poem can be seen with generosity assuring glory in heaven, but generosity would have been vital to the survival of small agricultural communities in the ancient Germanic and Norse worlds. A homestead might be rich one year but poor the next. By sharing with those less fortunate during times of plenty, families would be more likely to receive help from richer neighbours in the years that were poor.

The Old Norse Rune Poem gives the line *'Wealth is a source of discord among kinsmen'*,[76] which reminds us of the problems that wealth can cause between people. The next line *'The wolf lives in the forest'* gives a hint of the problems and anger that wealth can bring. Yet, if we look at the words again we can see another meaning. The discord among kinsmen is the worry that Fehu brings. Fehu needs protecting from negative outside influences; it needs protecting from others; it needs protecting from that which will reduce it. The wolf lives in the forest waiting. Does Fehu bring the wolf or simply intensify the fear of the wolf by giving us something we feel we must protect?

Fehu is sometimes linked with the grain harvest and with fertility, which leads many people to also link it with the Vanir gods Freyr and Freyja.

---

75 Galdrbok, Johnson & Wallis, 2005
76 Helrunar, Fries, 1993

Life lessons

Do we learn the lessons of Fehu more in poorer years, or in the years of plenty?

Times of poverty can teach us a lot about wealth that we thought we had, and that wealth is often transient. In a recession, stocks and shares and houses are worth less than they once were, reminding us that one good harvest doesn't always mean another will follow, and that a rich man is only rich while his goods are considered worth something. A rich man who has shared with others in their time of need is more likely to have friends to fall back on in his own times of need.

What does wealth actually bring us? How important is it?

Intoning Fehu

Feeeeeyuuuuuuuuuuuuuuooooooooh

Chanting Fehu reminds me of the sound of young cows mooing. The feeling from the energy is one of youth and freshness. The colour that I most associate with it is a golden yellow, like ripe corn, or the gold of a coin.

Fehu feels fresh and untainted. The rawness of the energy is bright and hopeful and has the ability to feed.

Using Fehu in galdr

The Fehu rune can be used to attract wealth. It can be used as a symbol in your wallet, or drawn onto payslips or bank statements. Due to its transient nature, Fehu on its own will not help you to keep your wealth or save for something over many years, but it will help you to attract the wealth needed for comfort and fun, or to help to pay bills that are due.

Fehu in divination

Runes should be read within the context of the question being asked, as well as the other runes around them. More details on using runes for divination are given in Section 4. Fehu appears in a reading, it often signifies wealth or money, but remember that the wealth it brings is transient.

URUZ – UR

*"The aurochs is resolute and horned overhead
Fierce and untamed, it fights with horns
That huge, proud, moor strutting beast"*[77]
Anglo-Saxon Rune Poem

*"Dross comes from bad iron
The reindeer often races over frozen snow."*[78]
Old Norse Rune Poem

Uruz, the aurochs, is often referred to as strength. Aurochs were large cows that are now extinct but lived in Europe until the 17th Century when the last one is thought to have died. In Scandinavia in the middle ages aurochs were domesticated. Aurochs were larger than domestic cows, measuring over six feet tall and were also known for their aggression. Hunting an aurochs was no easy task. Julius Caesar tells us that:

> *"The young men harden themselves with this exercise, and practise themselves in this sort of hunting, and those who have slain the greatest number of them, having produced the horns in public, to serve as evidence, receive great praise."*[79]

When we first consider the aurochs' association with strength, the first consideration has to be towards the sheer size and physical strength of the aurochs. Looking at the aurochs' history, we can also start to piece together another meaning, that of the endurance it takes to hunt an aurochs, and added to

---

77 Galdrbok, Johnson & Wallis, 2005
78 Helrunar, Fries, 1993
79 The Gallic War, Julius Caesar

that, the pride and bravado of the aurochs kill. Uruz then teaches us the immovable strength of the aurochs, but also the force and the strength of the aurochs hunt.

Jan Fries describes the shape of Uruz as the shoulders of the large aurochs.[80] I like to see Uruz as the shape of an upside down drinking horn. The drinking horn description gives us a link to the youths hunting the aurochs and claiming their horns as the prize. This leads us to see Uruz as a symbol of strength and pride, a badge of honour that shows that the wearer has achieved something impressive.

This gives us several meanings. The first is the sheer size and strength and immovability of the aurochs. Its power is in its size. The second meaning is linked to the endurance and courage it takes to hunt an aurochs. It is a rune for helping to continue a difficult project or to undertake a challenge. Finally, it is a symbol of achievement, something that shows prowess and bravery.

Life lessons

Uruz is those projects that seem to be moving but not at great speed. It is those challenges that we find most difficult. It is the things that take us the most courage to face up to and complete. Uruz is that which we choose to undertake not that which is thrust upon us. It is the things that we push ourselves to do in the face of fear, uncertainty, and the knowledge that it will be tough.

Intoning Uruz

Uruuuuuuuuuuuuzzzzzzzz

Uruz is intoned in a low note and sounds like a bull's call or like the low tones of a hunting horn. Uruz is strong and stable. The energy feels solid and unmoving. Jan Fries[81] in *Helrunar* gives the Uruz posture as standing leaning over with your hands swinging towards the ground. I think of Uruz as being a sturdy feet shoulder width apart martial arts immovable posture and

---

80 Helrunar, Fries, 1993
81 Helrunar, Fries, 1993

using this posture gives the feeling of Uruz standing ground and uncompromising.

Using Uruz in galdr

For confidence when dealing with other people (interviews, meetings with bank managers) mark Uruz on your stomach to give yourself the 'stomach' for the task, but to also encourage your audience to see your prowess and achievements and to therefore have more faith and confidence in you.

Freya Aswynn gives a description of drawing the Uruz rune in a glass of water and drinking it to encourage strength.[82]

Uruz is often included in the descriptions of battle and fighting runes.

Uruz in divination

Uruz in divination can mean several things. Often it can show up when there is likely to be a confrontation that you need to stand your ground within and gain respect. Other times it can represent a challenge that you have set yourself (often in describing the reason for the query). Sometimes I have seen it represent an initiation or a rite of passage.

---

82 Leaves of Yggdrasil, Aswynn, 1988

THURISAZ – THORN – THURS

"Thorn is very sharp for all warriors
Extremely grim and evil to grasp
For all men who settle in its mist."[83]
Anglo-Saxon Rune Poem

"Thurs causes anguish to women
Misfortune makes few men cheerful."[84]
Old Norse Rune Poem

Thurisaz in described in the Anglo-Saxon Rune Poem as being a sharp thorn.[85] A common description given of the rune is Mjollnir – the hammer of the god Thor. Thor was the god of thunder and the god most worshipped amongst the ordinary people. Thor angered easily and he was responsible for keeping the giants (*jotunn*) out of Asgard (the home of the gods).[86] Thor's hammer Mjollnir was said to have contained the essence of a giant and it was used to kill the giants that tried to invade. Thor can throw Mjollnir and it will always return straight back to him.

The Old Norse Rune Poem is interesting in that it says that (*'giant'*) causes anguish to women" followed by *'misfortune makes few men cheerful'*.[87] At first glance these two lines don't seem to fit together. If we consider giant as Thor's hammer and therefore as Thor's weapon it makes more sense as causing

---

83 Galdrbok, Johnson & Wallis, 2005
84 Helrunar, Fries, 1993
85 Galdrbok, Johnson & Wallis, 2005
86 Edda, Snorri Sturluson, Everyman translation. See Also The Penguin Book of Norse Myths, Holland, 1996
87 Helrunar, Fries, 1993

'*anguish*' to women. It would be interesting to look into the word '*anguish*' and see if the meaning of the Norse word can be read in other ways. My suspicion would be that this is actually a sexual reference, which makes the following sentence '*misfortune makes few men cheerful*' make a lot more sense.

Thorns bring to mind the tale of sleeping beauty trapped in the castle surrounded by thorns. The sleeping beauty myth bears a lot of similarities to the myth of Siegfried and Brunhild[88] and the '*kiss*' at the end of the story is often interpreted as being sexual and an antidote to the bleeding that put her to sleep originally. Indeed, thorns themselves can be seen as a euphemism for the phallus. As well as the sexual connotations, thorns are sharp and keep out intruders. They protect by attacking indiscriminately. They attack anything that gets close plus the person being protected needs to make sure they watch out themselves. Likewise, Thor's hammer takes a lot of handling, a hammer than returns always to its host needs the thrower to be ready to catch.

Life lessons

Is attack the best form of defence? How much damage do you do to those around you when protecting yourself physically or mentally? Who gets caught in the crossfire? Thurisaz is the sudden argument that comes from feeling vulnerable. Thurisaz is the pub fight caused by jealousy and pride. Thurisaz is the impulsive action that is meant to protect that which you feel needs protecting but ends up jeopardising it instead.

Intoning Thurisaz

Thor–eeeeeeeeeeeeeeeeeeeeeeessss-az

Thurisaz is a scream as much as an intonation. Sudden and shocking it reverberates around echoing back to the caller. The energy ricochets while the rune is intoned and then drops suddenly leaving an adrenaline rush and a feeling of foreboding. The emotional feel of this energy fills you with the sense that

---

88 The Saga of the Volsungs, Penguin

this rune is not one for everyday use and a very powerful tool when your need is great.

Using Thurisaz in galdr

As discussed, Thurisaz is a strong rune to use, perhaps the most powerful of all the 24. It is very much an *'in emergencies'* rune, used when your need to protect yourself and your loved ones outweighs the negative aspects.

First and foremost, Thurisaz protects. It protects in a sudden, unfettered attack that doesn't discriminate. Thurisaz can be used within an intimidating situation where you feel physically in danger from others. This is predominantly its best use. Intoned out loud when in physical danger it does two things, firstly it creates the foreboding feeling we have discussed earlier and suggests to your attacker that they should turn away and run. Secondly, shouting runes in public places singles you out to be someone that is possibly unstable and therefore better left alone!

Thurisaz can be used to protect people and buildings. This is a very strong protection, although indiscriminate. A row of thorns will protect you from the outside but it might keep away those who you would welcome, or more importantly, like sleeping beauty, it has the side effect of keeping you unable to get out. If you are looking for a protective rune, Algiz is a gentler, but no less powerful alternative.

Thurisaz can be used as a long distant attack. This is not as effective as an in-person attack because it is impossible to work out when it has arrived at its required location (and therefore when Thor's hammer will be returning to its sender). A Thurisaz returning to sender without proper care and attention will produce a counter attack not sent by the victim but by the sender. Thurisaz won't teach the attacked any lessons and more importantly, is unlikely to change anything for the positive. If you are experiencing enough anger and despair to consider using Thurisaz from afar then it is more beneficial to work on making the other person see why you feel the way you do (Hagalaz) and to work on making yourself feel calmer and more rational (Ansuz).

Thurisaz in divination

This is usually a warning, either against acting in anger yourself, or against the anger of others. It is sometimes indicative of watching out for difficult situations. It is also sometimes a warning that someone is harbouring anger towards you that they are likely to act on at some point. More usually, I have found, it is a warning against you to avoid impulsive actions that might cause you problems.

Thurisaz in readings is often a catalyst to problems in that a person simmering with worry about the actions of another might have a Thurisaz appearing to warm them against acting rashly. They mistake this as their worry being justified and that the person they are concerned about is really a cause for concern which causes them to attack out of worry and vulnerability, which is the reason Thurisaz appeared, warning them against this action.

Ansuz – Os – Oss

"Mouth is the shaper of speech
Wisdom's prop and wise men's comfort
And every peer's ease and hope."[89]
Anglo-Saxon Rune Poem

"Oss is the way of most journeys
But a scabbard is of swords."[90]
Old Norse Rune Poem

Ansuz is representative of the god Odin. It is often described as wisdom or communication. The Old Norse Rune Poem talks about an estuary which is often translated as mouth of the river which links in with the speech of the Anglo-Saxon Rune Poem[91] and means that the rune is often given the meaning of *'mouth'*. The Old Norse Rune Poem talks about the scabbard to the sword[92] which gives the suggestion of the mouth being as much a container as a tool for speaking.

Ansuz can mean clear thinking and intelligence. It is the wisdom required to approach a problem from another angle or the common sense that allows you to see the path through your problems. Ansuz is often described as the ability to communicate with others, either through speech or writing. Through meditating I also get the feeling that it represents that which contains higher wisdom. For example, you can use it to

---

89 Galdrbok, Johnson & Wallis, 2005
90 Helrunar, Fries, 1993
91 Galdrbok, Johnson & Wallis, 2005
92 Helrunar, Fries, 1993

speak to your subconscious, or use it to talk to deity. Ansuz can even be linked to conversation with the higher self.

Life lessons

Ansuz is the foresight to see what actions you need to take to lead you to where you need to be. It is the ability to see what you need rather than what you want. It is the best advice given at just the right time. Ansuz is the right decision taken through careful consideration and the sense of calmness felt through treading your feet on the right path, but also the nagging doubt when you are on the wrong path.

Intoning Ansuz

Oaaaaaaannnnnnsuuuuuz

Ansuz is bright and clear and rings pleasantly through the air. It vibrates within the throat and feels very connected with above. Its overriding emotion is that of calm contemplation and it brings the feeling that all is right with the world.

Using Ansuz in galdr

Ansuz can be used to help you make decisions. It is the best rune for meditating on a decision or a problem. Chanting Ansuz is also good for seeing the other side of an argument and for harnessing what is the best course of action. Ansuz is good to work with when you want to take emotion out of a decision and encourage rational thinking.

Ansuz in divination

Ansuz in divination will often be representative of something important. It often shows that a decision is correct or incorrect (depending on the runes around it) and forecasts life fulfilling or life changing events. Ansuz rarely appears as a warning; instead it shows decisions that have already been made or events which are unchangeable and important to the life of the questioner whether those have already happened, are imminent, or are far into the future.

The appearance of Ansuz alongside an event often shows something that isn't changeable because it brings the questioner to the place they need to be. Ansuz in thrown rune spreads will often appear right at the corner of the spread away from the other runes. This will usually represent that the question and the actions of the questioner have moved so far from their original plan that they are not fulfilling the original need.

RAIDO – RAD – REID

"Riding in the hall is soft for warriors
Yet hard when seated upon a mighty horse
Covering the mile paths."[93]
Anglo-Saxon Rune Poem

"Reid is said to be the worst thing for horses
Reginn forged the finest sword."[94]
Old Norse Rune Poem

Raido is said to represent a journey. The Anglo-Saxon Rune Poem talks about how *'Riding in the hall is soft'*[95] but that covering the miles or journeying a long way from home is difficult. The Old Norse Rune Poem is less clear and tells us that *'(riding) is the worst thing for horses'*[96] then talks about the forging of a fine sword. Jan Fries talks about Raido as being a quest or a journey to seek and retrieve something.[97] He explains that Raido can be seen as a soul journey or a shaman's journeying to the other worlds.

The rune poem descriptions of Raido discuss horses, but in such a way that suggests that it is a journey that the horses would rather not take - bringing us to question whether the journey Raido describes is more reminiscent of Siegfried's journey to Hel in the *Volsunga Saga*[98] than a journey across land. Intuitively, it seems as though Raido is a journey of the

---

93 Galdrbok, Johnson & Wallis, 2005
94 Helrunar, Fries, 1993
95 Galdrbok, Johnson & Wallis, 2005
96 Helrunar, Fries, 1993
97 Helrunar, Fries, 1993
98 The Poetic Edda, Snorri Sturluson

mind as in a pathworking or astral travel rather than a journey travelling on a horse.

The last two lines in the Anglo-Saxon Rune Poem are talking about difficulty and distance, does Raido in that case also signify difficult journeys?

Life lessons

Raido is the dream of a journey; it is the thinking about somewhere better. Raido is the feeling one gets when *'the grass is greener on the other side'* and when one wants to be elsewhere without understanding what they want to achieve. Raido feels very much like the seeking and the journeying rather than the outcome.

Intoning Raido

Raaaaaaaaaaiiiiiiiiiiiiid-yo

Raido is a clear, higher pitched sound that resonates in the head and in the crown chakra. It feels distant and unreachable. The energy that it brings is less of the journeying itself but more of the longing for what is at the end as though Raido is more about the seeking than the arriving. This fits in with Fries' feeling that Raido represents a quest.

Using Raido in galdr

Raido is often given as a talisman to people who are undertaking a journey. With Raido feeling more like an astral journey we can use it to unlock the fetters that keep us bound to Midgard and help us with astral travelling. Brian Bates in his novel of an Anglo-Saxon sorcerer[99] tells the story of someone that needed to be freed from his body in order to journey the worlds. Raido could be used in a similar way.

Raido in divination

Freya Aswynn refers to Raido appearing in a reading as often representing a warning that the path you have chosen is

---

99 The Way of Wyrd, Bates, 1983

not correct.[100]   I have found Raido to often be directional, pointing out a way the seeker is going, or joining two runes together in a path, pointing out the way that the reading needs to be read and piecing the rest of the story into a whole. Raido can often also represent a question or a yearning and hint at the source of the seeker's question.

---

100 The Leaves of Yggdrasil, Aswynn, 1988

KENAZ – CEN – KAUN

"Torch is familiar by its quickening flame
Pale and bright it burns most often
Where princes rest, inside."[101]
Anglo-Saxon Rune Poem

"Kaun is fatal to children
Death makes a corpse pale."[102]
Old Norse Rune Poem

Kenaz is fire. The Anglo-Saxon Rune Poem describes it as the flaming torch and says that it is clearly identifiable to all creatures by its fire.[103] The Old Norse Rune Poem describes it as *'fatal to children'*[104] which gives a slightly different meaning to the Anglo-Saxon Rune Poem possibly suggesting that Kenaz represents a disease or illness rather than fire itself. We can take the poem literally in that fire is fatal to children, or we can look on the Kenaz fire as being the healing. Fire can be used to purify and remove disease, either by removing the diseased flesh itself in the case of gangrene and infection, or by using heat to clean.

In my experience, Kenaz feels purifying and cleansing and I can easily think of Kenaz as an intense way to heal or to clear. Like fire, it burns away that which is diseased or infected or needs clearing to make way for the fresh. As a torch we can see Kenaz as being able to show that which is hidden in the dark. Freya Aswynn suggests that it comes from the same root as the words *'ken'* - *'to know'* and cunning. It shines the light on what

---

101 Galdrbok, Johnson & Wallis, 2005
102 Helrunar, Fries, 1993
103 Galdrbok, Johnson & Wallis, 2005
104 Helrunar, Fries, 1993

is hidden and gives knowledge of that which is not clear on the surface. Kenaz can see what motives are hiding.

Fire is both positive and negative. Fire gives us light and warmth and helps us cook. Fire that is left out of control can hurt and burn. Using fire to heal an infected wound is the last resort and destroys healthy flesh with the diseased.

Life lessons

Kenaz is the sudden realisation that there has been something discussed and implemented without your knowing. Kenaz is the discovery of a betrayal that you didn't see coming. Kenaz is the turning your back on something that you know does not have enough positive to save. Kenaz is the trap that catches the mouse or the nuts and seeds that draws the mouse out of hiding. Kenaz is the clever questioning that finds the guilty.

Intoning Kenaz

Keeeeeeeeeeeynaaaaaz

Kenaz is strong and loud and resonates in your chest and heart. It feels cleansing and helps to clear a space. It feels very final and safe, like a locked door. It feels like a freshly vacuumed and cleaned room.

Using Kenaz in galdr

Kenaz can be used to clear a room psychically. It works by seeking out that which is hiding. In my experience it is like shining a lighted torch around the space, scaring things out of their hiding place and sending them running out.

Kenaz in divination

Kenaz appears often to show that something is not the way it seems. Kenaz is often the warning that people mistake Thurisaz appearing in a reading to be. Kenaz shows you hidden motives and warns that below the surface plans are going on without you and are not necessarily what they seem.

GEBO – GIFU

"Giving is for men, noble and worthy
And for outcasts and others without means
A sustenance, support and an honour."[105]
Anglo-Saxon Rune Poem

Gebo is a gift. The *Havamal* tells us that a gift must be reciprocated.[106] To the Norse it was the mark of a good man to be generous, but every gift must be an exchange and in return the receiver must give a gift in return. The Norse honour also extended to welcoming travellers (in return the traveller would regale the householder with tales) and to respect and memories of the ancestors.

The idea of needing to make sure that everything was a proper exchange extended to a concept called Wergild. Wergild was the name given to the tithes that a person must pay to the family of anyone he killed in a dual (or otherwise). A man may challenge another and fight him to the death but the safety and comfort of his family should not have suffered for it. Wergild was the duty of care that Norse society gave to widows and descendants and it was considered very important.

The rune Gebo simply put means a gift. If we look further the term gift is more of an exchange, therefore Gebo reminds us that in order to get something we need to put something back. There is no shame in asking a fair price for one's work, however, there is a shame in not paying what you can afford for something. If we look at Wergild the expectation of Gebo goes further than this. It reminds us that every action has an

---

105 Galdrbok, Johnson & Wallis, 2005
106 Poetic Edda, Snorri Sturluson

outcome and that everything we do needs to be justified and paid for and that magic and religion works no differently.

Gebo can also be seen as an agreement. It is an interesting aside to consider that those who can't write have within even our recent history been asked to agree to things by marking an X which looks remarkably like a Gebo rune.

Life lessons

Gebo is the competition that you put lots of effort into to enter and win through hard work and ability rather than luck. Gebo is raising money through working rather than winning the lottery. Gebo is the coffee that you ran out of shop clutching in the hope that the seller didn't realise they forgot to charge you, only to find that you left your purse on the counter. Gebo is the favour that you owe your friend. Gebo is the karma that means that those who look after other people when they are upset will always have a friend in their times of need.

Intoning Gebo

Gaaeeeeeeeeeeeeeffffffoooooooooo

I believe that Gebo resonates better in the Anglo-Saxon (Gifu) than in the Germanic. Gebo resonates through the throat. It presents a sense of righteousness but above all feels peaceful and comfortable. It is homely and warm.

Using Gebo in galdr

Gebo can be used to invoke your share of an exchange where you feel you have been unfairly treated. Gebo is the trading standards of the Norse world and is great for making sure that you are not out of pocket unjustly. Gebo is used to invoke Wergild, ensuring that debts of all kinds are paid. If you are using Gebo in this way, make sure that your actions in the situation, and others, have been infallible as you might end up losing out elsewhere.

Gebo is a good rune to use when working with the gods. When you ask for something, let the gods know what you plan to give them in return and use Gebo as the signing seal in order to ensure that you both keep up your ends of the bargain.

Using Gebo within bindrunes that you have created for a specific magical want gives them the get out clause of *'a fair exchange'* and *'working for the good of all'*.

Gebo in divination

Gebo is the mark of an agreement. In divination it often represents a new exchange between people such as a new job, or a new friendship, or the sale of a house.

Wunjo – Wynn – Wenne

"Joy tolerates little of woe, sorrow or anxiety
For he that has for himself
Happiness and bliss
Amidst a town of plenty."[107]
Anglo-Saxon Rune Poem

"Wenne he enjoys who knows
No suffering, sorrow or anxiety,
And has prosperity and happiness
And a good enough house."[108]
Old Norse Rune Poem

The standard meaning of Wunjo is often given as *'Joy'*, which makes it a difficult rune to get in touch with as joy can be a fairly abstract concept. The word joy conjures up images of elation and celebration. Wunjo itself seems to feel more like comfort and contentment. It is a comfortable living without important needs or deep sadness.

Freya Aswynn tells us the root of Wunjo might be more likely to have come from perfection rather than joy,[109] thus conjuring up images of correctness and an absence of problems. Jan Fries suggests that Wynn is close to the word *'win'* and therefore Wunjo represents winning or the elation and celebration that come with winning.[110] Fries also suggests that Wunjo has a sexual energy to it and suggests that the posture of Wunjo is lying on the back with knees up and feet flat on the floor (in right angles) which gives the impression of a sexual win.

107 Galdrbok, Johnson & Wallis, 2005
108 Helrunar, Fries, 1993
109 Leaves of Yggdrasil, Aswynn, 1988
110 Helrunar, Fries, 1993

Certainly, when intoning Wunjo the energy centre that resonates corresponds to the sacral chakra, the energy centre below the belly button. This idea fits with all of the concepts of perfection, joy, and contentedness if we consider Wunjo to be the point after orgasm, the *'win'*. The *Havamal's* description of the sixteenth rune backs up this impression if we consider that this might be the stanza that talks of Wunjo

> *".... When all sweetness and love*
> *I would win from some artful wench,*
> *Her heart I turn and the whole mind change*
> *Of that fair armed lady I love."*[111]

This gives us the impression of winning over someone that isn't so enamoured originally, of *'taming the shrew'*.

Could we also see Wunjo as a seduction rune? Could it be used to bring the feelings of joy and peace and contentment into other areas of our life?

Life lessons

Wunjo is the feeling of a warm house while the snow falls outside. Wunjo is the afterglow of sharing a warm bed with an even warmer partner. Wunjo is the seduction you never thought you would fall for, and the smugness of the morning after.

Intoning Wunjo

Vaaauuuuuuuuuneeeoooooooohhh

Wunjo resonates the sacral chakra and has a medium low note. It brings feelings of contentment and comfort and the afterglow of orgasm.

Using Wunjo in galdr

Wunjo can be used to attract a partner. It isn't used to trick or mislead, but rather to create a feeling of comfort, safety, and sexuality around the person that has it marked upon them. Wunjo can be used to calm and bring about feelings of elation

---

111 The Poetic Edda, Snorri Sturluson

and contentment for short periods of time. For this reason, Wunjo can be very good for helping you to fall asleep.

Wunjo in divination

Sometimes Wunjo represents a partnership or shows that the question is about love and relationships. It is occasionally a rune that appears in order to show the reader what the question is about and set the scene. More often, Wunjo appears in a *'happily ever after'* setting in order to show that everything that is being worked towards is reaching its natural conclusion and that things will be settled and happy.

ᚺ

HAGALAZ – HAEGL – HAGALL

"Hail is the whitest corn
It swirls aloft
Tumbles in gusty winds
Then turns into water."[112]
Anglo-Saxon Rune Poem

"Hagal is the coldest grain
Christ created the world of old."[113]
Old Norse Rune Poem

The Hagalaz rune represents hail and is considered, along with Thurisaz, to be one of the most powerful runes of attack in the elder futhark. Hail is destructive in that the speed at which it falls can cause damage (especially to crops). Hail rattling against the window sounds almost aggressive and menacing, it makes itself far more known than even the hardest rain and the rune Hagalaz does the same. The Anglo-Saxon Rune Poem tells us that it then *'turns into water'* which gives us a clue about the way in which the Hagalaz rune interacts with us. Often the effects of the Hagalaz come and go suddenly, blending back into the background of our lives as though nothing ever happened.

The Old Norse Rune Poem tells us that *'hail is the coldest grain'*[114] and this is an interesting statement in that it is almost suggesting that Hagalaz acts as a grain, only it is one that cannot be ground into food. The sudden downfall of hail is reflected in the way that sometimes Hagalaz is representative of a sudden change and problem in life which can cause a huge

---

112 Galdrbok, Johnson & Wallis, 2005
113 Helrunar, Fries, 1993
114 Helrunar, Fries, 1993

amount of distress and discomfort before disappearing as though it had never happened.

Jan Fries suggests that Hagalaz also represents the winter[115] and the way that winter meant the slowing down of life in Norse society. The depths of winter were so cold that it was impossible to farm, or to travel so families would be together in their home, with only each other for company and the work they could do from home. Any supplies they had collected with the harvest would have needed to last for the entire frost period. Hagalaz therefore traps someone with their thoughts. As the winter is a time for reflection, Hagalaz becomes a time for someone to think about their actions and the consequences. Hagalaz is a time for reflection and a time when lack of preparation might cause need. Hagalaz is the start of the winter, the first thoughts and worries and the first falling of hail and the turning of the year. Hagalaz gives way to Nauthiz which highlights the lack of supplies and health which in turn gives way to Isa which is the waiting for the spring.

Life lessons

Hagalaz is the action that leaves you alone and wondering. Hagalaz is the long car journey that leaves you stuck on the motorway for hours and thinking about the past over and over again. Hagalaz is the sudden disaster that leaves you reeling but leaves behind peace and a new understanding with no lasting damage. Hagalaz is the sick realisation that your actions in the past must have led someone to feel as bad as you feel now.

Intoning Hagalaz

Haagalaaaaaaaaaaaaaazz

Hagalaz is screamed rather than intoned, very much like Thurisaz. It is a hard rune that seems to shake and rattle around the room and almost takes you by the shoulders and shakes you. It feels bleak and harsh. It shocks and leaves

---

115 Helrunar, Fries, 1993

behind it a numb feeling as though all the warmth and energy in the room has been sucked out.

Using Hagalaz in galdr

Hagalaz can be used as a form of attack which makes it a similar rune to Thurisaz. It is much better to use in a long distant attack than Thurisaz because it is a more introverted rune in that it gives the person an opportunity to think about things and learn from them. In that way, a Hagalaz attack can be a far worse experience than a Thurisaz attack which is often quick and stunning but with few emotional side effects. A Hagalaz attack is more beneficial in other ways because it allows the person to learn from their mistakes. Hagalaz acts as a psychic *'go to your room and think about what you have done'* in the way that it creates a situation that allows contemplation and remorse. Like many of the other runes, you need to be absolutely sure that you are blameless before using this rune.

Hagalaz in divination

Hagalaz comes up frequently in divination as a period of contemplation. It often reflects that the questioner is considering their actions and wondering what they can do about making amends. Hagalaz also represents a period of aloneness or a period of study that doesn't automatically mean that it will be difficult.

NAUTHIZ – NYD – NAUDR

"Need, like a stretcher about the breast
Thought oft as a mortal sign, can augur well
Help and heal, if attended to quickly."[116]
Anglo-Saxon Rune Poem

"Need gives scant choice
A naked man is chilled by the frost."[117]
Old Norse Rune Poem

Nauthiz follows on from Hagalaz and represents need and want. It is often described as a rune that talks about hardship and hunger and indeed Ralph Blum and those following his work give it as one of the runes they consider to be a negative rune.[118]

I think of Nauthiz as following on from Hagalaz and representing the next stage of winter when the initial shock of the coldness and being indoors gave way to the realisation that you needed to make your stocks last and to prepare for a long spell in relative hardship. In the early days things are rationed until it becomes clear that the wait is nearly ended when planning is easier.

The Norse winter was a difficult time, but it was a time of necessity and rationing was self imposed. While I was in Sweden a few years ago a friend told me of a folk tale that a certain rock was where the older people of a village used to jump from at the beginning of winter. This of course is unthinkable to our modern day culture, but he explained that if they knew that

---

116 Galdrbok, Johnson & Wallis, 2005
117 Helrunar, Fries, 1993
118 The Book of Runes, Blum, 1984

it was unlikely that they would last the hardships of winter then it was fairer to not use up the food that other people could enjoy. This puts into perspective the Nauthiz rune because it becomes less of a gamble whether or not you will get through to the other side, but a definite that you will or you would not have undertaken the challenge. Hunger and need brings a certain drive that allows important work to be done and gives a determination to succeed that might not have been within a comfier time.

Freya Aswynn suggests that Nauthiz is a rune that allows you to learn from mistakes.[119] Nauthiz therefore follows on from Hagalaz as the period of time after the initial understanding which allows you to piece together what has happened and ensure that the same doesn't happen again.

Life lessons

Nauthiz is the point at which you are forced to take action on an ongoing negative situation. Nauthiz is the drive that keeps you planning to avoid a certain situation from happening again. Nauthiz is the careful planning that allows you to undertake challenges such as climbing mountains or sailing.

Intoning Nauthiz

Neeeeeeeeeeeed

The Nauthiz rune is one of the few that I prefer to intone in its Anglo-Saxon name. Nauthiz is intoned in a quiet mid range rumbling tone that vibrates in the chest and stomach. The energy feels empty and very similar to the numb feeling that comes after Hagalaz. It is subdued and small and feels very much like closing in or like the feeling that comes before you pass out.

Using Nauthiz in galdr

Nauthiz is a difficult rune to in galdr. It is either used as a softener for the Hagalaz rune (when used in conjunction with an attack) or it is used to stop damaging behaviour such as

---

119 Leaves of Yggdrasil, Aswynn, 1988

addiction. It brings things down to the bare bones and allows growth upon them.

Nauthiz in divination

The Nauthiz rune is often considered to be a negative rune within divination. Very often it does suggest a need to slow down and rethink or to start learning the lessons we are being given. This does not have to be seen as a bad thing. Nauthiz is the turning point within a damaging situation and a call for action. It should be seen as the help coming rather than feared.

ISA – IS

"Ice is exceedingly cold, very slippery
Glistens like glass, much like a jewel.
Floor frost, fair-wrought, a fine sight."[120]
Anglo-Saxon Rune Poem

"Is we call the broad bridge
The blind man must be led."[121]
Old Norse Rune Poem

The Anglo-Saxon Rune Poem talks about the beauty of ice. It is slippery and cold, yet it is beautiful like glass.[122] The danger of the ice is almost eclipsed by the beauty of it. The Old Norse Rune Poem talks about the ice as a bridge and explains that the blind man must be led.[123] The Anglo-Saxon Rune Poem is perhaps easier to understand than that the Norwegian. The solid ice is something that isn't as scary as it could seem. The poem gives the rune a positive slant. The Old Norse Rune Poem[124] seems to be saying that the ice can be walked across. By freezing on top of the water the ice gives us access to areas that we might have not been able to go before. The ice forms a bridge. Yet the blind man must be led because the ice is still dangerous despite being useful.

Isa follows on from Hagalaz and Need as the third stage of winter. To me Isa represents the end of winter, the last cold

120 Galdrbok, Johnson & Wallis, 2005
121 Helrunar, Fries, 1993
122 Galdrbok, Johnson & Wallis, 2005
123 Helrunar, Fries, 1993
124 Helrunar, Fries, 1993

spell before the ice begins to thaw and make way for the first signs of spring. Isa is therefore a rune with a positive outlook. Isa is the time when the worst is over and the wait for spring seems to be shorter. Isa is the time when the worst of the rationing is hopefully over and we know how much food we need before spring.

Isa like ice holds things in standstill. It is a still quiet time and grabs onto life and keeps it solid and stable. For some things this is helpful but in others it can be stifling. Isa can also be used to hold onto memories, to freeze the beautiful and keep them safe within us like the solid ice keeps things frozen and the same beneath it. Isa preserves. It keeps fresh that which we need to keep fresh for as long as we need it to.

Life lessons

Isa is the visits to places we knew as children that seem never to change. Isa is the hope that comes from knowing that the end of a difficult time is not far away. Isa is the wait for spring or for something that we have been planning for. Isa is the house or job that we don't seem to be able to leave no matter how hard we try.

Intoning Isa

Iiiiiiiiiiiissssssaaaaaaa

Isa is clear and plain, ringing out far and wide like an alarm. It is a higher note that resonates in the mind. The tone is unchanging between the syllables. Isa brings calmness and a sense of knowing that everything will be ok. Isa invokes memories of the past and the need to hold on to what is dear to us.

Isa in galdr

Isa is used to prolong the inevitable, to hold onto it and keep it for longer than it has planned to be. In some situations it can be used to try to prolong life for a short while, for example to ensure that someone can meet with their loved ones a last time before they die. It can be used to push a difficult situation that is looming (such as the repossession of a house) further away in order to buy more time to find a way to stop it. It can be used by people with long-term degenerative diseases to try and give them more time before the disease takes hold.

Isa in divination

Isa in divination will most of the time work with the runes around it. It can show where a blockage is occurring or it can hint at time spans.

JERA – GER – AR

"Year brings hope for men
When gods in heaven
Permit the earth to give forth
bright crops for rich and poor."[125]
Anglo-Saxon Rune Poem

"Ar is a boon to men
I say that Frothi was generous."[126]
Old Norse Rune Poem

Jera is often described as the earth or as Nerthus the goddess of the earth. It is also referred to as the harvest. The Anglo-Saxon Rune Poem discusses the bringing forth of shining fruits from the earth[127] and the Old Norse Rune Poem talks about plenty and generosity.[128] Frothi was a Danish King who was renowned for his benevolence.[129] The mention of bright crops in the Anglo-Saxon Rune Poem gives us the idea of the healing warmth of the sun and the beauty of the earth and the plants.

Jera continues on from the runes Hagalaz, Need, and Isa as the three stages of winter. Jera is the birth of spring and the time of plenty. It is the time when fruitfulness returns to the earth and food is once more fresh. Jera as well as being fertility and beauty and fruitfulness therefore also has an element of recharging the batteries and of healthiness. From the months of

---

125 Galdrbok, Johnson & Wallis, 2005
126 Helrunar, Fries, 1993
127 Galdrbok, Johnson & Wallis, 2005
128 Helrunar, Fries, 1993
129 The Cult of Kingship in Anglo Saxon England, Chaney, 1970

eating dried and preserved food and rationing, the spring and summer bring fresh fruit and vegetables which give the health a fresh boost as does the reappearance of the sun.

Jera is also the time to step outside again and to pick up projects where they have been left. Jera is a time of hard work and achievement as well as fruitfulness. Jera is also the turning of the year. Its shape is cyclical and explains that Jera is the turning of time which sometimes gives it the explanation of being time itself.

Life lessons

Jera is the project that we have discovered the key to finishing. Jera is the new health routine, the diet and gym membership that makes us feel good about ourselves. Jera is the first strawberry.

Intoning Jera

Yeeeeaaaaaaaaarrrraaaaaaaahhh

Jera is a celebration. The sound is mid range high and resonates in the chest. It brings a sense of fulfilment but also a sparkling energy that makes us want to try new things and take on the world.

Using Jera in galdr

Jera can be used to increase harvests of all kinds, whether that is a harvest of a new project or whether that is harvesting fruit and grain. A secondary use for Jera is to add energy. It can help to kick start a project or help to combat lethargy in a person or lethargy for a project or task. Freya Aswynn suggests that Jera can be used to speed things up or reach a resolution quickly[130] therefore working in the opposite way to Isa which slows things down.

Jera in divination

Jera in divination represents abundance. It shows that something will be successful and hints at a healthy harvest. In

---

130 Leaves of Yggdrasil, Aswynn, 1988

its spring context it shows an end to hardship and difficulties. It can also suggest that a healthier diet or lifestyle is necessary.

EIHWAZ – EOH

"Yew is outwardly an unsmooth tree
Hard, fast in the ground, a keeper of fires
Roots writhing-beneath a joy on homeland."[131]
Anglo-Saxon Rune Poem

"Yr is the greenest of trees in Winter
It is wont to crackle when it burns."[132]
Old Norse Rune Poem

Eihwaz traditionally is described as representing the Yew tree. This has led some to associate it with Yggdrasil, the world tree[133] which although most commonly described as an Ash tree has also been suggested to be Yew. Yew trees are thick, evergreen trees that are often associated with death due to the way that they are often planted in graveyards. The Yew is also poisonous, which is possibly another reason why it is associated with death. The Old Norse Rune Poem tells us that the Yew tree is the greenest of trees in winter, remarking on its evergreen nature. The Anglo-Saxon Rune Poem tells us that it is a tree that stands hard and fast in the earth[134] which reminds us of its solidity. It also says that it is a guardian of flame. The link with fire is echoed in the Old Norse Rune Poem.[135]

Yew was used to make longbows. This imagery makes sense in terms of the Eihwaz rune when you think about the shape of

---

131 Galdrbok, Johnson & Wallis, 2005
132 Helrunar, Fries, 1993
133 Leaves of Yggdrasil, Aswynn, 1988
134 Galdrbok, Johnson & Wallis, 2005
135 Helrunar, Fries, 1993

it. Looking at the bow shape and the description of Eihwaz in the rune poems as Yew we can consider the idea that Eihwaz represents the longbow. Certainly, chanting Eihwaz brings the feelings of a call for help. It reminds me of an alarm bell or a hunting horn. It feels like a call across the air to say *'come and help me'* or like lining up comrades to fight beside you.

Although the following *Havamal* stanza is near to the beginning of the section that discusses the runes, I feel that perhaps Eihwaz is the rune that it is describing:

> *"Those songs I know, which nor sons of men*
> *nor queen in a king's court knows;*
> *the first is Help which will bring thee help*
> *in all woes and in sorrow and strife."*[136]

Life lessons
Eihwaz is the argument that you hope as many people as possible will take your side on. Eihwaz is the realisation that you need to make a stand and you hope that people will stand with you.

Intoning Eihwaz
Eiiiiiiyyywaaaz
Eihwaz is intoned on a long even note. It sounds like a hunting horn or like a warning bell. It is a sound that rings out. A call to arms, it feels like it is helping to gather support towards you.

Using Eihwaz in galdr
Eihwaz can be used to gather together support for a cause. It is also one of the runes that can be used as protection. As a protection rune it sits between Thurisaz and Algiz. Thurisaz protects with indiscriminate attack. Algiz protects with strength and security and with the *'do not cross'* aspect. Eihwaz fits somewhere between these two runes in that as the longbow it

---

136 The Poetic Edda, Snorri Sturluson

threatens that it can attack and if needed can gather an army, but it doesn't attack indiscriminately like the thorns of Thurisaz.

Eihwaz in divination

Eihwaz often appears in order to remind the questioner that they are not alone. In a similar way it appears to show that a concern that they want to raise or an action they are about to take will be supported.

PERTHO – PEORTH

"Peorth is unfailing recreation and laughter
When spirited warriors sit blithely together
Riddling in the beer hall."[137]
Anglo-Saxon Rune Poem

The meaning of the rune Pertho is much debated. Many rune workers[138] have given this rune the traditional meaning of fate or of chance and games. Some have even linked it to gambling. Blum refers to Pertho as the dice cup linking it both to gaming and to chance. The Anglo-Saxon Rune Poem says Pertho is *'unfailing recreation and laughter'* and talks about warriors in the beer hall.[139]

Freya Aswynn is very clear in her belief of Pertho being one of the birth runes and points out the possibility of a mistranslation in the Anglo-Saxon Rune Poem[140] which changes *'warriors in the banqueting hall'* to *'wives in the birth hall'*. Those that believe Pertho to be about birth liken Pertho to the shape of a womb. In regards to the Anglo-Saxon Rune Poem, perhaps discussing the warriors blithely sitting together in the banqueting hall is a euphemism which rather than deals with the wives helping to give birth, describes the warriors sitting in the beer hall awaiting the news from the birth hall.

Regardless of what was the original terminology used in the Anglo-Saxon Rune Poem, Pertho to me feels instinctively more about birth than about games of chance. However, if we look at birth in Norse society we can see that there was a bit more

---

137 Galdrbok, Johnson & Wallis, 2005
138 Mostly those working from Ralph Blum, see the Rune Cards, Blum, 1995
139 Galdrbok, Johnson & Wallis, 2005
140 Leaves of Yggdrasil, Aswynn, 1988

chance and gambling involved in this than in our society. Birth is always a difficult and dangerous process, even now, but post birth was also a life or death situation for a Viking baby.[141] When a baby was born it was taken immediately from its mother (before its first feed) and presented to its father. If its father claimed it as his own he named it and the baby was taken back to its mother for a feed and to live a happy, provided for life. If it was not claimed by its father it wasn't allowed to do this. Under this understanding the warriors waiting has almost as much significance to the birth of a child as the midwives do.

In this case it is easy to see Pertho as much as representative of fate and wyrd as it is representative of birth. Pertho the meaning is therefore both birth and chance. It is the fate and gamble associated with whether a baby is claimed or not by its father. The game of chance that is absolutely associated both with wives in the birth hall and with warriors in the beer hall.

Pertho's shape is often compared to a dice cup or womb.[142] Jan Fries suggests that it could also refer to a birthing posture[143] and gives this posture as a squatting posture. Looking at childbirth in Norse society this is not a standard posture used for birthing. However, Jenny Jochens' study[144] of Norse birth gives us the standard birthing pose which is remarkably familiar. This is on knees and hands making a bridge shape, which then moves to knees and elbows once labour is fully established. The elbows and knees pose from the side gives us a shape that doesn't take any imagination to consider as being the shape of the Pertho rune.

Life lessons

Pertho is the dreams and hopes for the future life and path of your unborn child. Pertho is the chance you take that throws yourself at the mercy of the decisions of others. Pertho is the

---

141 Women in Old Norse Society, Jochens, 1995
142 The Book of Runes, Blum, 1984
143 Helrunar, Fries, 1993
144 Women in Old Norse Society, Jochens, 1995

life path that you take that doesn't feel like you made the decision but were guided by what had to be done.

Intoning Pertho

Peorrrrrrrrrth

Pertho is a guttural low sounding note that resembles the noises made by a woman in labour. It is one of the runes that I feel resonates best using its Anglo-Saxon name (Peorth). The emphasis is on the OR note. It is reminiscent of birth but also brings the feelings of anticipation and waiting for a decision. There is the element of pause that accompanies the announcement of the winner of a competition, the pregnant pause.

Using Pertho in galdr

Pertho can be used to work with and/ or alter the path of fate. It can be used to help you see the web of wyrd and make life decisions that will take you where you need to go. Pertho is one of the runes used for childbirth. It is used for turning chance the right way, taking away elements of childbirth that can go wrong easily. Pertho (along with Berkana) can be painted onto the womb during labour. They can also be painted onto the palms of the birthing partners who then clasp their painted palms to the hands of the birthing mother channelling the energy for the runes through them and into the birthing mother.

Pertho in divination

Pertho is a rune that usually appears in conjunction with other runes. It appears when a situation is an important one and often points out the correct action to take. Interestingly, it doesn't seem to represent birth literally in most readings.

ALGIZ / ELHAZ – EOLH – YR

"Elk sedge oft inhabits fenland
Growing in water, it grimly wounds
And burns with blood any man who grasps it."[145]
Anglo-Saxon Rune Poem

The Algiz rune traditionally[146] represents a certain kind of rushes. The Anglo-Saxon Rune Poem refers to it as Elk Sedge and describes it as growing in the marshes and within water.[147] Jan Fries describes this as a kind of grass with sharp edges that cut when walked upon.[148] The shape of the rune is reminiscent of the splayed leaves of a rush or of the antlers of an Elk. The marsh is an area that is inhabitable for many and is sometimes dangerous to cross and to inhabit. This means that marshes have a lot of folklore and mystery surrounding them,[149] especially within East Anglia which is the area of the United Kingdom with the most marshland. Fenland stories talk about witches and faeries living in the marshes and describe them as a gateway between the worlds of faerie and the worlds of the living. A marsh is neither land nor water in the way that dusk is neither day nor night and this gives it the feeling of being a boundary.

Although most rune workers agree that Algiz represents the elk sedge, I have always been given the picture of Algiz within pathworkings and meditations as a large, protective Oak tree

---

145 Galdrbok, Johnson & Wallis, 2005
146 As seen in the Rune Poems and also Freya Aswynn, Jan Fries, Ralph Blum
147 Galdrbok, Johnson & Wallis, 2005
148 Helrunar, Fries, 1993
149 The Old Stories, Holland, 1997

which is the symbolism that I most often use for it. Its arms are strong and protective, keeping you away from and hidden from passing danger and solid within its branches. The Oak tree is solid and strong and has been standing for generations offering peace and protection. Algiz, to me, feels fatherly, like a strong male energy, but one that can also be stifling, as strong male energy is often stifling in order to protect from harm. There is an additional rune in the Anglo-Saxon futhark (Ac) that has been given the association of Oak.

We can find comparable feelings from the traditional meaning of Algiz if we look at the meaning of Algiz as marsh rather than as Elk grass. The marsh to those who lived within and around it was a safe place to be simply because it was so difficult to cross. Crossing the marsh after dark was something that was fraught with danger and therefore something that wasn't attempted unless there was an emergency. This meant that those living where it was impossible to reach without crossing the marsh were safe, at least after dark, if not during the day. The marsh keeps you away from passing danger and the rushes keep you hidden from it. Just like the Oak tree. The marsh, just like the Oak, has been standing for generations, and offers peace and protection. The one difference is that traditionally, as something so associated with water, the marsh would be representative of a strong female energy. However, the link with the Oak is that the marsh in itself is stifling in that it protects you from the outside but also makes it very difficult for you to get out, which also gives it that parental feel.

Interestingly, Algiz is the one protection rune that is discussed in the rune poem as being able to cause pain and harm. Its use to me feels safer and less attacking than both Eihwaz and Thurisaz. Possibly this is because of the separation and the barrier that it gives you. Thurisaz is a hedge of thorns that intruders can see a way through (and also the hammer that is thrown indiscriminately). Eihwaz is the warriors that stand ready to attack one by one. Algiz is the barrier that is clear that you can't cross. It protects without attack because only the foolish would attempt to get close enough to be hurt.

Life lessons

Algiz is the parent that keeps you safe but doesn't allow you to break out and find your own way through the danger. Algiz is the arms that you return to for comfort and security. Algiz is the problem that you hide from and allow to pass rather than face head on. Algiz is the place that you avoid or the people that you automatically put a barrier against because you don't want to get close to them.

Intoning Algiz

Aaaaaaalllllllgiiiiiiz

Algiz is intoned in three parts the *'a'*, the *'llll'*, and the *'giz'*. It is a clear but solid sound in between a low tone and a mid tone. It brings the feelings of safe arms around you, of being supported, and of being ultimately safe and secure. Occasionally it can feel over protective.

Using Algiz in galdr

Algiz is ultimately used to protect. It can be drawn onto houses or a row of Algiz runes drawn across fences, windows, and doorways to protect your space. It is a good rune to intone before you sleep if you want to sleep feeling safe and protected. It is a good rune for personal protection to be marked on your body when you feel unsafe.

Algiz in divination

Algiz appears in divination within its protective mode. It often shows what part of their life the questioner feels vulnerable within. I have often seen Algiz appear in readings to show that the questioner's personal protection (or the people that protect them) is constrictive and need to be more fluid.

SOWILO – SIGEL – SOL

"Sun for seafarers always gives hope
To those who ferry over the fishes bath
Til their sea stallion brings them to land."[150]
Anglo-Saxon Rune Poem

"Sol is the light of the world
I bow to the divine decree."[151]
Old Norse Rune Poem

Sowilo pure and simply represents the sun. If we look culturally at our thoughts of the sun we see it as offering light and warmth but of being damaging when it is too hot. We are also coloured by our view that the sun is the centre of our universe and that it is essential for the growth of plants and that we need the sun to create vitamin D but that too much can give us skin cancer.

The Anglo-Saxon Rune Poem talks about the sun as a guide that helps seafarers find their way home.[152] This is something that has ceased to be so important to our society but was essential within the early medieval society. This element of the sun, pointing out the way home, helps us to see what the rune Sowilo could be used for.

The Old Norse Rune Poem says that the sun is divine and the light of the world.[153] This is far closer to the meaning that at first glance we would assume the rune to have. In Norse

---

150 Galdrbok, Johnson & Wallis, 2005
151 Helrunar, Fries, 1993
152 Galdrbok, Johnson & Wallis, 2005
153 Helrunar, Fries, 1993

mythology the sun is female, driven across the sky in a chariot by Sol. The return of the sun in the Norse lands, as we saw from the Jera rune, melts the ice and encourages the return of the grass, corn, fruits, and flowers. It brings back life, fertility, and fruitfulness. Within the United Kingdom a lack of sun during the dark half of the year can cause all kinds of health problems most notably the seasonal depression known as SAD (Seasonal Affected Disorder), which comes about through lack of sunlight. In hospitals in the early part of last century UV and light therapy was considered essential to encouraging healing. Even today jaundiced and premature babies are given light treatment to encourage their bodies to grow and heal.

These examples give us a range of meanings for Sowilo. The first is as a guide. The sun is able to show you your way home and to help you to find the right way to go. The second is for adding energy and growth to a project. The energy of Sowilo added to a magical working can bring growth and add an extra level of energy and push to the outcome.

The third use of Sowilo is within healing. Sowilo can be used to help bones, tendons, sinew, and skin to heal itself. Like any kind of magic it should never be used instead of modern healthcare and medicine but can be a helping hand towards it. For example, a broken leg will not heal in the correct place unless it is secured in a plaster cast, but Sowilo alongside the plaster cast (or drawn onto the plaster cast) can help the bones to heal quicker. Sowilo can help the body to heal itself within a faster time frame.

Life lessons

Sowilo is the first warm days of springtime. Sowilo is the energised exhaustion that comes after physical exercise. Sowilo is the teacher that facilitates your learning. Sowilo is the things you need to recover from a difficult time.

Intoning Sowilo

Soooooweeeeeeeluuu

Sowilo is a rich clear tone that is intoned at mid level. It vibrates the heart and has the emphasis on the middle syllable.

Sowilo is a warming feeling, like the sun on your skin on a summer day. Sowilo brings feelings of healing and calm but also the pricklings of energy that brings you thoughts of all the things you need to do and motivates you to get started on them.

Using Sowilo in galdr

We have already suggested that Sowilo can be marked onto the casts of broken bones. It can be intoned and drawn upon any bruises, fractures, or sprains in a similar way, to encourage the body to heal itself. Sowilo can be used within a spell to add energy. Sowilo can be chanted when lost to allow the Sowilo rune to help to calm you and guide you peacefully to where you need to be.

Sowilo can also be used to kick start something that you have been working on that is as yet to *'bear fruit'*, i.e. a project that is waiting to become successful that you have been working hard on.

Sowilo in divination

Sowilo often appears to show where a questioner has been concentrating their energy. It can also appear within a thrown rune set to show that it is not around any other runes and therefore the energy that is being put into life by the questioner is not hitting where it is supposed to and needs better channelling.

Sowilo also appears in order to guide the questioner towards the right path. It points to where it needs to be. Sowilo will also appear to represent a teacher or someone that will help the questioner to learn. Sowilo can also represent growth and fertility but this is often reflected because of the energy that the questioner has put into a project rather than being representative of the growth itself.

TIWAZ – TYR

"Tiw is a clear dependable sign
Keeps steady with princes, is ever on course
And never wanders over the night mist."[154]
Anglo-Saxon Rune Poem

"Tyr is a one handed god
Often has the smith to blow."[155]
Old Norse Rune Poem

Tiwaz represents the god Tyr. Tyr is said to be the god of justice and of sacrifice.[156] One myth about Tyr discusses the time when the gods of Asgard needed to bind and fetter the mighty wolf Fenrir.[157] The only way to do this was to trick him into stepping into a harness that had been charmed with magic to make it strong. Fenrir was suspicious of magic because the harness looked so harmless so Tyr promised him that he would put his hand into his mouth as proof that they should be trusted. Of course when Fenrir realised that he had been tricked and that the binding was strong enough to keep him trapped, he bit down and Tyr lost his hand. This is why Tyr (rather than Odin) was said to have been the god of sacrifice.

It is not too much of a leap to link Tyr with the god that Tacitus talks about in *Germania*,[158] Tuisto, who he says is a sky god and the main deity for the Germanic lands. This leads some

---

154 Galdrbok, Johnson & Wallis, 2005
155 Helrunar, Fries, 1993
156 Asyniur, Women's Mysteries in the Northern Tradition, McGrath, 1997
157 The Penguin Book of Norse Myths, Holland, 1996
158 The Germania, Tacitus, Penguin Classics

authors[159] to suggest that perhaps at one point Tyr was the head of the Aesir pantheon rather than Odin. Tuisto had a son called Mannaz which is the name of another rune in Tyr's Aett. Tyr's link with justice always strikes me as more of a *'what must be'* as much as the justice of balance. Sacrifice comes from the willing sacrifice that Tyr made in order to fetter Fenrir the wolf and to keep the gods safe.

The Old Norse Rune Poem clearly discusses Tyr's sacrifice.[160] The second line I interpret as meaning that the blacksmith (the person responsible for amputating limbs) often needs to make the final blow. The sacrifice of a limb to stop the infection spreading is a hard one to make. The amputation of a limb for reasons of justice (for example punishment for stealing) links the line in with justice as well as sacrifice. The Anglo-Saxon Rune Poem on the other hand links Tyr with a guiding star[161] (possibly the North Star?) keeping faith with princes and guiding through the mists of night. It is interesting to consider how this fits in with what we know about the god Tyr. It links in far more with the information we have about Tuisto the sky father than the Norse mythology that remains.

Life lessons

Tiwaz represents the actions that we take knowing that they will cause us harm or sadness in the short-term in order to take us where we need to go in the long-term. Tiwaz is the sacrifices you take in order to make someone you love happy, knowing that it will hurt you. Tiwaz is the need to ensure that things are done properly. Tiwaz is the need to feel that people need to learn from their actions.

Intoning Tiwaz

Teeeaaar

Tiwaz is another of the runes that seems happier to me in its Anglo-Saxon name (Tir). Tiwaz is intoned on a mid to low note with the emphasis very slightly on the end of the word. It

159 Asyniur, Women's Mysteries in the Northern Tradition, McGrath, 1997
160 Helrunar, Fries, 1993
161 Galdrbok, Johnson & Wallis, 2005

conjures up feelings of determination and the strength and bravery that comes from knowing that this is the only way forward, whatever the consequences.

Using Tiwaz in galdr

Tiwaz can be used in conjunction with Hagalaz in order to make sure that someone learns from their actions and that justice is done. Tiwaz can be used to add weight to a legal dispute that you are 100% sure that you should be the victor of. When using Tiwaz you need to remember that Tiwaz lines up with justice rather than the party that has invoked it so you need to know for certain that you are in the right by the eyes of the law before you take this action. When using Tiwaz, don't forget that the majority of what Tiwaz stands for is sacrifice for greater good. Are you willing to make this sacrifice? Are you sure what this sacrifice might entail?

Tiwaz in divination

Tiwaz can often represent a difficult decision. It reflects a situation where perhaps the best course of action is the one that looks as though it is going to cause problems. It is essential that Tiwaz is read in combination with the other runes in the spread and the actions that each one can bring considered. Tiwaz can also show up a difficult emotional situation where the questioner is still considering whether the decision was the right one.

BERKANA – BEORC – BJARKAN

"Birch has no fruit
Bears shoots with no seed
A leaf laden crown amidst high shining branches
Delightful garland aloft in the sky."[162]
Anglo-Saxon Rune Poem

"Bjarkan has the greenest leaves of any shrub
Loki was fortunate in his deceit."[163]
Old Norse Rune Poem

Berkana is the Birch tree. The Birch tree is often said to have a traditionally feminine quality and to be associated with healing and with childbirth. The Anglo-Saxon Rune Poem discusses the height and magnificence of the tree and that it doesn't bear fruit but reseeds by growing suckers.[164] Suckers grow off of the base of a tree and can be taken and replanted elsewhere, growing into full trees over the years. However, Birch trees do produce seeds and fruit, which leads some people to think that the Anglo-Saxon *beorc* translates as Poplar rather than the Birch, although some species of Birch tree also produce suckers. The reseeding through suckers is possibly where the association with birth comes from with this rune.

The Old Norse Rune Poem talks about *Bjarkan* as having the greenest leaves, and follows with a discussion about Loki's fortunate deceit.[165] The green leaves remind us of the fertility of the Birch. The line below I believe is talking about the myth where Loki becomes a mare in order to distract the horse of a

---

162 Galdrbok, Johnson & Wallis, 2005
163 Helrunar, Fries, 1993
164 Galdrbok, Johnson & Wallis, 2005
165 Helrunar, Fries, 1993

giant and allow the gods to win a bet.[166]   As a result of this *'distraction'* Loki the Mare became pregnant and gave birth to a horse with eight legs called Sleipnir who became Odin's horse. This would give the stanza an express link with birth.

Meditating on Berkana it feels calming and numbing.   It gives a different kind of calm to some of the other stress relieving runes such as Ansuz or Wunjo. Berkana's calm is a deeper calm soothing from a deeper place; it is a maternal calm as though it can hold us close with memories of the womb. Echoing this maternal calmness is the shape of Berkana, which resembles breasts. Berkana's numbing effect reminds us that the Birch tree has sometimes been associated with anaesthetic. Its numbing effect feels like a form of pain relief and this is something that we can use Berkana for. Considering Berkana as representing the Poplar we can also look to the way that the Poplar is used to reduce fever or as an antiseptic.

Life lessons

Berkana is the peace of a relaxing massage. Berkana is the lullaby that you use to sing a child to sleep peacefully. Berkana is the hot drink and blanket before you go to bed. Berkana is the hot lemon drink that relieves the symptoms of your cold.

Intoning

Berrrrrrrrrkaaaaaanaaaaaa

Berkana is a low quiet tone that has equal emphasis on all syllables.   It is a haunting and comforting sound vibrating through your stomach and reminding you of feeling at home and safe.   It feels supporting and pain relieving.   Berkana also reminds you of the emotion you feel when comforting a crying child.

Using Berkana in galdr

Berkana is a great pain reliever of both emotional and physical pain due to the calming effect it has. Intoning Berkana gives someone in pain something to focus on and imbues them

---

166 The Penguin Book of Norse Myths, Holland, 1996

with the feelings of peace and maternal love that come from chanting the Berkana rune. This is the reason why Berkana is so good for relieving pain and stress within childbirth. Berkana is a good rune to use in order to calm a crying baby. It calms and takes the anxiety away from the worried parent as well as creating a sound that invokes the primal feelings of peace and security echoing the peace and security of the womb. Berkana is also a great rune to chant when you need to feel safe and secure or need help sleeping.

Berkana in divination

Berkana's association with birth means that often it is described as representing birth, growth, and new life.[167] I have found that it deals more often with motherhood rather than birth which may not seem like a big difference but instead of the literal meaning of a new baby or the meaning of a new project, Berkana represents the feelings and emotions of looking after someone else and being responsible for their wellbeing.

---

167 The Rune Cards, Blum, 1995

EHWAZ – EH

"Horse is for nobles, a princely joy
Horses hoofing proudly where
Wealthy riders bandy words
A steed to the restless, is ever a comfort."[168]
Anglo-Saxon Rune Poem

The traditional meaning of this rune, as we can see from the rune poem is that it represents a horse. If you look at the shape of Ehwaz then it can be described as two horses with their heads facing each other.[169] The Anglo-Saxon Rune Poem talks about Ehwaz as being a *'joy to princes in the presence of warriors'* and suggests that it is a comfort to the restless.[170] The straightforward reading of this would give us the idea that princes can ride away quickly from warriors when on horseback and that the restless can ride miles away on horseback or use horses for entertainment.

Some rune workers consider Ehwaz to be movement and transport, taking a leap from horses being used as transport and therefore giving the meaning of Ehwaz as movement, journeying, and quite often as travel. It is worth remembering that the Norse did not solely use horses for transport and that they did have chariots[171] therefore long distance travel or travel that involved moving lots of people and belongings would have been done using chariots.

Ehwaz, the horse, comes after Berkana, birth. If we remember that the line in the Old Norse Rune Poem talks of Loki giving birth to Odin's horse Sleipnir the order of the runes

---

168 Galdrbok, Johnson & Wallis, 2005
169 Futhark, Thorsson, 1984
170 Galdrbok, Johnson & Wallis, 2005
171 The Penguin Book of Norse Myths, Holland, 1996

becomes significant to the meaning of Ehwaz. What if Ehwaz represents a specific horse, Odin's eight legged horse Sleipnir? Freya Aswynn[172] also draws the conclusion that it is likely that Ehwaz represents Sleipnir. The link to Odin's horse takes the movement and travel element a step further as there are several accounts describing Odin as riding Sleipnir across the nine worlds, more specifically, to Helheim.[173] This links in with the practise of seidr and witchcraft.

Freya Aswynn goes on to point out that horses were used for divination[174] and that they were also linked to witchcraft and seidr as nightmares and niding poles. Within Norse saga literature a nightmare was a woman who could leave her body astrally travelling as a horse[175] and visited men while they dreamt and 'rode' them to death. A niding pole was a stick with a horse's skull on it that was used for cursing.

Life lessons

Ehwaz feels so linked with witchcraft and seidr that its lessons seem to be represented outside of everyday life and associated specifically with feminine magic in the Northern tradition.

Intoning Ehwaz

Ehhhhhhwaaaz

Ehwaz is another of the runes that sounds more like a scream than an intonation. (Hagalaz and Thurisaz are the other two) There is equal emphasis on both syllables. Its energy feels very much like seidr and very otherworldly. It is a strong, feminine rune. Ehwaz energy feels very much outside of you.

Using Ehwaz in galdr

Ehwaz can be used for astral travelling or for sending an astral message to someone. Another use of Ehwaz is when journeying specifically to Helheim. It can be chanted while

---

172 Leaves of Yggdrasil, Aswynn, 1993
173 The Poetic Edda, The Edda
174 Leaves of Yggdrasil, Aswynn, 1993
175 Heimskringla (Ynglinga Saga), Snorri Sturluson

making an astral journey to Helheim or marked onto someone to help them journey. Riding an Ehwaz rune (through visualisation or by drawing the rune onto a piece of paper for you to sit on whilst you journey) is another way of using it to transport you.

Ehwaz in divination

Ehwaz can represent the need for action when dealing with a person or situation. It is also very connected with the world of the dead (Helheim) and therefore sometimes comes up for those who work as mediums or as seidr workers in order to point out that someone wants them to make contact with them. The rune Othala can occasionally stand in for Ehwaz in this situation but almost always just represents family members, therefore a message from the grave is far more likely to appear in a reading as the Ehwaz rune.

MANNAZ – MAN – MADR

"Man in his glee is dear to his kin
Though each must betray his fellows
When the drihten decrees
The pitiful flesh condemned to the earth."[176]
Anglo-Saxon Rune Poem

"Man is the augmentation of the dust
Great is the claw of the hawk."[177]
Old Norse Rune Poem

The question over the Mannaz rune is whether it represents Man as in Male or Man as in Mankind.[178] The Anglo-Saxon and the Old Norse Rune Poems are ambiguous. The Anglo-Saxon Rune Poem seems fairly negative in its reckoning that *'each must betray his fellows'* before describing man as pitiful flesh to the earth, a rotting corpse.[179] The Old Norse Rune Poem discusses man as being an augmentation of the dust,[180] which we can read as perhaps referring to the brief amount of time that man lives for, his slight disruption of the dust of the earth before he dies of old age. The claw of the hawk is another line that we can read into Norse mythology. Loki, in the guise of a falcon, took the goddess Idunna away from the Aesir.[181] Idunna was the goddess who had the golden apples of youth which the Aesir ate in order to stay young. When Idunna was gone, so were her apples and the gods of Asgard began to grow old.

---

176 Galdrbok, Johnson & Wallis, 2005
177 Helrunar, Fries, 1993
178 Helrunar, Fries, 1993
179 Galdrbok, Johnson & Wallis, 2005
180 Helrunar, Fries, 1993
181 The Penguin Book of Norse Myths, Holland, 1996

If we read the second line of the Old Norse Rune Poem in this way we see that it is discussing the briefness of man's life. Great is the claw of the hawk that takes youth away from us. In this manner, the Anglo-Saxon Rune Poem line *'every man is doomed to fail his fellow'* sounds less about treachery and more about a fellow not being able to stop death.

The link to the preceding rune, Ehwaz, being representative of the feminine mysteries of witchcraft and seidr could lead us to draw the parallels that translate Mannaz as being about traditionally male mysteries but Mannaz seems less about maleness and more about the fragility of mankind. Mannaz is two Wunjo runes facing each other. If we see Wunjo as being the peace that comes from sex and orgasm (*'la petit mort'* – the little death), then is Mannaz the peace that comes from la grande mort, death itself? Mannaz then in representing the human race can also be seen as representing the fear of mankind of the end of life. In this way, the link to Ehwaz could be seen as Ehwaz faces the dead whereas Mannaz waits for it with its back turned.

Life lessons

Mannaz is the realisation that life is for living and loving. Mannaz is the death of someone close to us. Mannaz is the significant birthday that makes us consider the aging process.

Intoning Mannaz

Moaaaaaaaanaaaaaaaazzzz

Mannaz is a mid note that vibrates within the heart. It feels strong and solid, grounded in the earth like a big tree. It feels connected to life and to history.

Using Mannaz in galdr

Mannaz can be used to combat depression. It reminds you of the shortness of life and of the importance of living it to the full.

Mannaz in divination

Mannaz can often signify that the questioner has been thinking about their life and their part in society. It can signify that the questioner is either thinking of, or has been, securing their continuation through history by achieving something that will be important. Its link with death can also mean that it can signify an initiation or rite of passage.

LAGUZ - LAGU – LOGR

"Water to folks seems never ending
To him who must venture on an unsteady ship
While high waves terrify
And the sea stallion heeds not the bridle."[182]
Anglo-Saxon Rune Poem

"Logr is a river which falls from a mountain side
But ornaments are of gold."[183]
Old Norse Rune Poem

Laguz represents a great expanse of water – a sea, a river, a lake, a waterfall. I would go further than this to say that as Kenaz embodies the element of fire, so Laguz embodies the element of water. The Anglo-Saxon Rune Poem discusses the ocean as a huge thing that is never ending with terrifying waves.[184] The Old Norse Rune Poem talks about Laguz as the waterfall, a river that falls from the side of a mountain.[185]

Various assumptions have been made about the rune Laguz. The first is that it is linked with feminine and with the emotions.[186] This idea has come from the western belief that the element of water is connected with the emotions and traditionally feminine values. The second is that it is linked to the god Njord who is the Norse god of the sea shore, or the goddess Nerthus who is often associated with Njord. To me, the traditional values of the element of water that Laguz holds are

182 Galdrbok, Johnson & Wallis, 2005
183 Helrunar, Fries, 1993
184 Galdrbok, Johnson & Wallis, 2005
185 Helrunar, Fries, 1993
186 Rune Rede, Grimnisson, 2001

those of purification and the ability to neutralise and cleanse. The link it has with emotions seems to be in its ability to clear emotions or to clear the energetic residue that is often associated with high emotions.

Although most people describe Laguz as a feminine rune it seems to me to be more asexual. Its ability to cleanse and clear gives it a sterile feeling that seems unable to support the distinction that would allow it to have a defined gender, considering that male and female are very much assumptions based on our opinions of what constitutes male or female.

Life lessons

Laguz is the bath that allows you to think things over fully meaning that you emerge peaceful and bereft of the thoughts that were previously spinning round and round your mind. Laguz is the mixture of salt and water that purifies a space.

Intoning Laguz

Laaaaaaaagooooooooooz

Laguz is a high note with the emphasis on neither syllable. It holds the same note throughout. It vibrates the third eye and feels very cleansing and sterilising. It feels calming in the way that it removes the worries from your mind. It feels like a freshly cleaned house.

Using Laguz in galdr

Laguz can be used to purify a space. Like a tidal wave or a waterfall it flushes through neutralising emotional and psychic residue. Freya Aswynn says that Laguz can be used to get people to carry out reasonable requests for you.[187] Possibly the reason for this is because Laguz removes the unnecessary emotions (such as pride or dislike or jealousy) that would usually stop a person from following out that request.

---

187 Leaves of Yggdrasil, Aswynn, 1988

Laguz in divination

Laguz within divination is another rune that it is essential to read in combination with the other runes. It often refers to the fact that the questioner is working on high emotion and therefore needs to take a step back and think rationally before making any moves or decisions.

Inguz – Ing

"Ing was first seen amongst the East Danes
Til he departed over the waves
His wagon following behind him
Thus the hardy man named that hero."[188]
Anglo-Saxon Rune Poem

Inguz represents the god Ingvi Frey[189] who was a fertility god, associated with the fertility of the fields and the fertility of people. Ingvi Frey was often depicted as having a large erect phallus. The Anglo-Saxon Rune Poem talks of Ing being driven in a wagon and departing over the waves.[190] This stanza can be read as telling us that Ing was a god worshipped by the East Danes but that his worship spread with the migration of his followers east across the waves. A rite used to help fertilisation of the fields and a good harvest was to pull a statue of Freyr, who is often associated with both Ingvi Freyr and Ing, with a large phallus around the fields in a chariot.[191]

The description of the rune as the god Ing gives us a link with fertility and growth. The shape of the rune heightens this as it is representative of both the penis and of the vagina.[192] It also bears an uncanny resemblance to DNA. It could also be said that it represents a sheaf of corn. The question over the meaning and use of Inguz is whether it represents fertility (including the fields and the harvest), human fertility, or sexuality. My hunch is that it is representative of sexuality and conception rather than of generalised growth and fertility (for

---

188 Galdrbok, Johnson & Wallis, 2005
189 Helrunar, Fries, 1993
190 Galdrbok, Johnson & Wallis, 2005
191 The Gods and Myths of Northern Europe, Davidson, 1969
192 Leaves of Yggdrasil, Aswynn, 1988

this is represented by the Jera rune). Inguz therefore represents both male and female genitals and the point of conception. Sexual attraction and relationships are linked with this but is more under the jurisdiction of the Wunjo rune. Inguz rather than attracting a partner ensures that the union is fruitful.

Life lessons

Inguz is the strength of magnetism that attracts you sexually to someone. Inguz is the desire within and for the sexual organs.

Intoning Inguz

Iiiiiiinguuuuuuuuz

Inguz is a low quiet tone with a slight emphasis on the second syllable. Inguz unsurprisingly vibrates the sacral chakra centre, between the belly button and pelvis. It brings feelings of arousal and desire for sex.

Using Inguz in galdr

Inguz is used for sexual attraction to bring about and heighten arousal. Inguz can also be used by those trying to conceive a child. Inguz can be chanted and/ or marked onto the phallus or at the point of the womb (on the stomach just above the pubic triangle. Inguz can also be used to conceive and manifest a new idea or project.

Inguz in divination

Inguz is almost always representative of sexual relationships. In those occasions where it doesn't represent this it can represent a new project that is at the seed stage, only just a concept ready to be planted and grown.

OTHALA - ETHEL

"Home is exceedingly loved by each man
If he may often enjoy its due rights
Happy at home, in prosperity."[193]
Anglo-Saxon Rune Poem

Othala is the rune that represents the ancestors and the family. It is often described as *'the homestead'* and Ralph Blum gives its meaning as inheritance.[194] The Anglo-Saxon Rune Poem talks about Othala as being home and talks about enjoying the house in constant prosperity.[195] In many ways Othala is about the home but its full meaning gives us far more than this.

Until very recently the eldest son, if not more of the children of a household, would not move out of the house they were born in. The house was the property of the family and it was expected that it was passed down as inheritance. The house would be shared by the family. The eldest son would inherit the house once his parents had died, but his children would be brought up in the house with their grandparents and the house would pass on to his eldest son. The house that you lived in would be infused with the memories (and often the possessions) of your ancestors. Stately homes would not only hold the memories and possessions of the owner's ancestors but they would also hold the portraits of them. Thinking about Othala in this way makes us realise that home and inheritance and ancestors are all associated.

---

193 Galdrbok, Johnson & Wallis, 2005
194 The Rune Cards, Blum, 1995
195 Galdrbok, Johnson & Wallis, 2005

To the Norse, kinship was very important. The stories of those who had passed on were told and retold in the belief that keeping the memory of someone alive helped to keep the person alive. It was important for the Norse that their actions and deeds would be something that people would remember them for and celebrate them for after their death so that their name and memory would live on.[196]

It was also considered that sometimes you might have to consult the ancestors in order to help you with decisions. This was done by visiting the grave mounds of the ancestors and spending the night sitting on them in order to return the next day with a greater wisdom. This was called *utiseta* or *'sitting out'*.[197]

Life lessons

Othala is the photo album that reminds you of childhood. Othala is your grandparents' stories of their childhood which links you with your heritage. Othala is the visits you make to castles and stately homes that are no longer lived in. Othala is the feeling you get when you walk through the front door of a house you love living in.

Intoning Othala

Ohthaaaaaaaaaaaaaaaaalla

Othala is in toned in a clear, high note. The emphasis is on the middle syllable. Othala brings an immense feeling of feeling at home. It also brings about memories of childhood and family associations.

Using Othala in galdr

Othala can be used to create instant feelings of homeliness. It is a good rune to use when you have just moved to a new house and it doesn't feel like your own yet, or when you have had something traumatic happen in your home that has stopped it feeling homely.

---

196 The Poetic Edda, Oxford World Classics
197 For more about utiseta see Nine Worlds of Seidr Magic, Blain, 2001 or Seidways, Fries, 1996

Othala in divination

Othala represents family and the home. Othala is almost always a rune that is associated with happy feelings and memories. Often Othala will represent an upcoming birth within your family, occasionally it might also signify death.

DAGAZ – DAEG

"Day is the drihten's herald, dear to men
Great Metod's light, a joy and a hope
To rich and poor – for all to use."[198]
Anglo-Saxon Rune Poem

Dagaz is translated as day. The Anglo-Saxon Rune Poem talks about day as being a herald, and equally beloved and of service to everyone rich and poor.[199] Sometimes the final two runes Dagaz and Othala are switched so that Othala is the final rune.[200] I prefer to have Dagaz at the end as I find that its meaning seems to encompass the fact that it is the last rune in the futhark.

Dagaz as well as representing the day time specifically represents the dawn. It might seem strange to have a rune meaning dawn and therefore beginnings at the end, but this is only if we look at the runes as linear. By seeing the runes as circular, Dagaz becomes the last rune and the first rune, the end and the beginning. Whereas in some New Age or magical beliefs we are reminded that all ends are also beginnings,[201] Dagaz reminds us that the new beginning comes as a result of the end of something else.

One lesson of Dagaz is that it is always darkest before the dawn. The dawn comes only after the coldest and darkest part of the night and likewise an illness or a problem or conflict is always at its height just before it starts to resolve itself. In the most Northern parts of Scandinavia at the height of summer the

---

198 Galdrbok, Johnson & Wallis, 2005
199 Galdrbok, Johnson & Wallis, 2005
200 Helrunar, Fries, 1993 and Galdrbok, Johnson & Wallis, 2005
201 For example, when reading the Tarot the Death card is about new beginnings as well as endings

days are very long and the sky never gets completely dark. The dawn is often the time when you realise that the sky has got dark because the slowness of the darkening sky means that it is easy to miss. The rising of the sun reminds you that the sky has darkened and of the time rather than the beginning of the darkness. Dagaz sometimes works like this in that a difficulty is only highlighted by the solving of the problem which comes upon you suddenly, releasing the news that there had been darkness.

Life lessons

Dagaz is the argument that shows you that there has been conflict for awhile without you realising. Dagaz is the day of an illness where you don't see how you can cope with the discomfort any more.

Intoning Dagaz

Daaaaegaaaaaz

Dagaz sounds new and bright and is intoned at a mid to high tone. It vibrates the crown chakra and brings feelings of warmth and hope. Dagaz energy does not however feel brand new, the energy is reminiscent of running a marathon in that the elation is the ending but the tiredness from the challenge still holds.

Using Dagaz in galdr

Dagaz can be used to speed things up that are moving slowly, including being used to force decisions to be made sooner. Dagaz can bring about the conclusion, thereby magically closing the door on something. I believe that Dagaz is the third rune that can be used within giving birth. Dagaz in galdr speeds up the inevitable or draws to a close something that has been lingering. This means that it can speed up a labour that has been in progress for too long, can speed up the last stage of labour, or can bring on labour in someone that is overdue.

Dagaz in divination

Dagaz represents an end and/ or a beginning. It can also represent an important decision that needs to be made or that someone is waiting on.

DO YOU KNOW HOW TO CARVE?

This section deals exclusively with making your own runes. There are a huge number of beautiful and magical rune sets available to buy, made by some very talented craftspeople (some of whom are also heathens). However, due to the simplicity of the shapes of the runes and the selection of tools and materials you can get hold of cheaply and easily, it doesn't take a lot of artistic talent to make your own set.

Chapter 8

MAKING YOUR OWN

When people buy runes, rather than make their own, you often hear them say that they want something that feels right, or more specifically, has been made by a heathen. The reason people want to ensure that their runes have the right kind of energy is twofold. The first thing that they want to make sure of is that their runes don't have any residual feelings or energies that will affect the readings and make them seem less accurate. This is a concern that perhaps has come from other divination practises, like Tarot cards and crystals, where it is important that they hold your energies and are cleansed of other people's energies regularly. With the runes, you are working with individual energies, and although these can be heightened by using materials that are complementary, it is difficult to use something or do something that will give an inaccurate reading.

The second reason you would want to make sure that someone who works with the runes has made your set (if you haven't made them yourself that is) is so the energy within them is magnified. You want your runes to feel energised and powerful when you hold them. Rune sets in some way will always be easier to charge than many other tools, simply because the energy is the rune itself so the simple act of marking the runic sigil onto your material energises it. However, there are other things that you can do to ensure that you harness more of the energy of the rune in your set.

Wanting your rune set to feel powerful and energised and to hold your energy is not the only reason why I believe it is important to make your own rune set. Perhaps the most important reason for making your own is that you learn a huge amount about the runes through making them. A big part of working with the runes is the act of carving and marking them and the lesson of putting the energy into the rune is an important one.

Sourcing the Right Materials for Your Runes

Size

How large you want your runes to be depends on how you plan to use them. Are you going to want to carry them round with you? If so, you don't want to use anything too large. Do you want to *cast* the runes by throwing them? If so, they all need to be able to fit in your cupped hands. How large do the sigils have to be in order for you to be able to see and read them properly?

Material

Rune sets can be made out of pretty much any material. Natural stone materials such as rocks, crystals, and pebbles, are all good for giving your runes that heavy stone like quality. Pebbles are very easy to find either in the garden, on the banks of streams and rivers, or on the beach. Crystals can be found in jewellery shops, both physically and online, as well as in New Age shops and the like. One advantage here is you can choose crystals based on the magical meanings traditionally given to them. You can even use a different crystal for each rune and match the energy according to the energy of the rune. If you choose hard natural materials like stones and crystals, you will need to use an acrylic or plastic based paint or varnish.

Wood is often considered to be the traditional material for making runes. Wood has the advantage that you can carve the runic sigils into it if you wish. You can leave the wooden pieces unfinished or you can sand and shape and varnish them. Wood, like crystals, has the added benefit that you can choose the wood with the symbolism you want to bring to your rune work. You might want to follow the observation of Tacitus and use the wood from a nut bearing tree.[202] If you are using wood that you have collected yourself from nature remember that some wood is easier to work with than others. Elder, for example, has a soft core which can make cutting the branches

---

202 The Germania, Tacitus, Penguin Classics

into chunks difficult. Ash is often chosen to make runes because of its association with Yggdrasil, the world tree, but this also can have a soft pithy core. If you are sanding and shaping the wood yourself, be very careful if you decide to use Yew as the wood is poisonous.

Shaped, finished, blank pieces of wood are easier to come across than you might think as they are often used for making things like magnets or pin brooches. There are online suppliers and craft shops that should be able to supply these to you fairly easily and cheaply.

Another material which is popular for making runes is clay. You can find a number of different clays that are easy to use at home and they have the advantage, like wood, of being able to carve the runes into them. Air-dry clay begins to harden when it is exposed to the air. Polymer clay (FIMO, Sculpy) is made with a percentage of plastic and is baked in a domestic oven. PMC or *'precious metal clay'* is made with a percentage of precious metal (usually silver) which means that the clay becomes metallic when baked. This material is expensive (c£25 for a piece big enough to make three or four runes) but will create a very special set.

MARKINGS

Most often the runes themselves are marked in red. There is a belief that the runes should be written in blood. This is something that many heathens continue although they tend to use either a drop (their own!) mixed in with another medium or something like menstrual blood which doesn't require a wound to acquire. Using blood mixes your energy with the energy of the runes. It is something that allows the runes to become more your own tool than something like the Tarot for example. If you are keen to charge your runes with your own energy, remember that the simple act of making (of choosing material, of painting, of carving) creates an energetic link. Also, don't forget that blood is not the only bodily fluid available to you when making your runes.

My first set of runes were made using menstrual blood (and a branch of an Elder tree) and do have a particularly strong feeling and energy about them. However, this might be as much to do with the fact that I made these runes over many months, learning and living with each rune until I felt comfortable enough with their energy to be ready to mark the rune. Any rune set created in this way, with this much energy put into them, will feel as strong.

Acrylic paint is an obvious choice as it works well with many different materials. Red nail varnish is easier to find than acrylic paint (and often cheaper depending on the brand) and comes with its own brush! Nail varnish is great because it is simple to use and is designed to coat something and stay in place. Making your own runes from ready shaped wood or bought crystals and nail varnish is a very easy way of creating runes and makes the materials accessible to almost everyone. Yet, the process of making these runes will teach you far more than buying a set will. Model making paint is another good choice for using on glass, stone, or crystal.

Resins like ochre and dragons blood work well when mixed with a clear varnish. Red Ochre powder is fairly difficult to get hold of, but well worth doing if you want to give your runes a primitive feel. Dragons blood resin is used in incense, which makes it slightly easier (although sometimes slightly expensive) to get hold of in powder form. Dragon's blood resin looks uncannily like blood and when mixed with a clear varnish (a clear nail varnish works very well for this) and goes onto the material fairly well. Dragon's blood ink (or any other ink for that matter) works well on unfinished wood, as it soaks into the wood.

SHAPE

Do you want your runes to all have the same shape or to be individual? Do you want traditional round or oval runes or something individual like squares (you could even go for stars or hearts or hammer shapes).

Tacitus[203] wrote about rune staves, therefore you could use sticks or staves. Twigs with the bark shaved off of one end look wonderful but lolly sticks work just as well. The benefit of using staves is that the runes interact with each other in a very fluid way during readings.

THE RUNES AND THEIR VOICES

You can use the chart below when making your runes to help you remember the order of the runes and their voices.

ᚠ	Fehu	*Feeeeeyuuuuuuuuuuuuuooooooooh*
ᚢ	Uruz	*Uruuuuuuuuuuzzzzzz*
ᚦ	Thurisaz	*Thor–eeeeeeeeeeeeeeeeeeeeessss-az*
ᚨ	Ansuz	*Oaaaaanssssuuuuuuuz*
ᚱ	Raido	*Raaaaaaaaaiiiiiiiiiid-yo*
ᚲ	Kenaz	*Keeeeeeeeeynaaaaaz*
ᚷ	Gebo	*Gaaeeeeeeeeeeffffffooooooooo*
ᚹ	Wunjo	*Vaaauuuuuuuuneeeooooooooohhh*
ᚺ	Hagalaz	*Haagalaaaaaaaaaaaaazz*
ᚾ	Nauthiz	*Neeeeeeeeeeeed*
ᛁ	Isa	*Iiiiiiiiiiisssssaaaaaaa*
ᛃ	Jera	*Yeeeeaaaaaaaaarrrraaaaaaahhh*
ᛇ	Eihwaz	*Eiiiiiyyyywaaaz*
ᛈ	Pertho	*Peorrrrrrrrrrth*
ᛉ	Algiz	*Aaaaaaallllllgiiiiiiz*
ᛋ	Sowilo	*Soooooweeeeeeeeluuu*

---

203 The Germania, Tacitus, Penguin Classics

↑	Tiwaz	*Teeeaaar*
ᛒ	Berkana	*Berrrrrrrrrkaaaaaanaaaaaa*
ᛖ	Ehwaz	*Ehhhhhhwaaaz*
ᛗ	Mannaz	*Moaaaaaaanaaaaaaazzzz*
ᛚ	Laguz	*Laaaaaaagooooooooooz*
ᛜ	Inguz	*Iiiiiiinguuuuuuuuz*
ᛟ	Othala	*Ohthaaaaaaaaaaaaaalla*
ᛞ	Dagaz	*Daaaaegaaaaaz*

MAKING YOUR RUNES IN AN AFTERNOON

As discussed previously, unless you feel specifically concerned about the material you are using to make your runes from, there should not be any reason to purify and cleanse your materials before you start, as the energy of the rune will cancel out anything not needed. However, if you are making all your runes in one sitting you might feel as though you want to put yourself and the space you are working in the right frame of mind. If this is the case, start by using the purification runes Kenaz and Laguz. By chanting first Kenaz and then Laguz you can make sure that there is no residual energy or feelings within the room or within yourself that might distract you.

Taking each rune in turn, intone the rune at the same time as you paint or carve the rune's sigil. The rationale behind this is that you become the channel for bringing the rune into the space you are working in. By marking you then create a gateway that allows the energy to enter your material. Visualise the energy of the rune being channelled through you and manifesting through the runic sigil and into your material. When marking your runic sigil you will find that often the amount of syllables in the voice can be matched to the strokes you need to make on the markings. Sowilo for example has three strokes to mark and three syllables. If this sounds really simple, it is because it is! This is one of the things that make runes such great tools to make. Any extra energy that you create within the material itself (by cutting, shaping, and finishing) will add to the strength of the feeling you get from your runes.

MAKING YOUR RUNES OVER 24 DAYS

(OR 24 MONTHS)

By giving yourself more time to work on each rune you give yourself more time to work with the energy of that rune directly, before needing to harness it into your rune. If you are serious about learning the runes and working with their energy, giving yourself at least 24 days to make your set really is the way to do it.

For each rune, take a day to attune yourself to it. You don't have to spend all day on working with the rune, but spend a significant amount of time throughout the day thinking about it. Wake up in the morning and intone the rune. Depending on how brave you are feeling (and what rune you are working with) you might also want to mark the rune somewhere on you. If you are taking 24 days then you want to use something washable as you will need to mark a new rune on you the day after. If you are taking longer than 24 days you could think about using henna to mark your rune and working on learning the energy of that rune until the henna has worn.

The reason that I say *'if you are brave enough'* is because by wearing the rune for a day you are asking it to live with you for that time (longer if you are using henna) and as such you are asking for the opportunity to learn the lessons of the rune through your daily life and through life lessons. In practise, this is a very good way to learn the runes and you will end up with a very strong insight into them. Reading through some of the life lessons of the runes, it might be that you don't want to invoke them into your life and would prefer to learn them indirectly through pathworkings, meditations, and other less immediate ways of experiencing the energy.

After you have marked the rune onto you, go about your daily business; reminding yourself every time you have a quiet moment, or every time you see the rune on you, what it represents. Later on in the day take some time out to work with the rune.

Find somewhere comfortable and away from other people enough to be able to intone loudly without feeling subconscious. Think about the shape of the rune and the traditionally given meanings. Intone the rune. Practise different kinds of voice until you find one that you are happy with (see chapter six). Intone the rune and feel the energy and emotions that it engenders in you. You can also journey to talk to the rune by using a pathworking (see chapter six).

Marking the rune should be the last thing you do before you go to bed. Before you start marking your rune, read the rune poems again (and if you like, also read the research that other rune workers have done) and think about the rune in accordance to your day. Has anything happened that has given you a greater understanding of the rune? Has anything unusual happened? What information did you gain from intoning the rune or journeying to meet it? Have you found a meaning that isn't spoken about elsewhere? Intone the rune as you carve / paint the sigil. You might find that you dream about the rune or that on waking, you have been able to decipher something else about its energy and meaning that you haven't before. If you keep a magical journal or a dream diary, you will automatically note it into this. If you don't keep one, make sure you find some way of keeping a record of this information.

ADDITIONAL EQUIPMENT

The two things that are very useful when using your runes are a bag to keep them in and some pieces of fabric to cast the runes onto.

There are several ways to mark your material. The easiest and most straightforward way is to get hold of some fabric paint (you can even buy fabric paint in the form of pens which are even simpler) and add your markings on that way. The other ways to mark your cloth are slightly more complicated but depending on your abilities and the equipment that you already use they are very achievable. The first is to use embroidery which gives a lovely homemade and very personal effect.

The second is to use an iron on t-shirt transfer. There are some available that you can print directly from your computer. These come in both A4 and A3 size (although that depends on the size of your printer). You can also buy pieces of silk that you can print straight onto from your computer. If you have an interest in stencilling or screen printing it is relatively simple to transfer shapes onto your cloth. The easiest way of all to create the target effect on cloth would be to cut out three circles of material and appliqué them onto your cloth one on top of the other using fabric glue or stitches.

You can make a bag to keep your runes without too much effort. Here are two very simple designs and one that requires a bit more skill.

Ribbon tie bag

Cut two rectangles of fabric. Basically, you want to draw out how big you want the bag and then add two inches to the top. With the fabric right side together, sew the rectangles up until the two inches at the top begins. Overlock or secure the edges of the unsewn sides of the fabric to prevent them fraying but don't sew them to each other. Turn down the top one inch which should leave you with a gap large enough to thread a piece of ribbon through. Do the same to the second edge. Secure by sewing but make sure that you leave a gap between the two and that you don't sew the top pieces of the bag together. Thread your ribbon through one side and then the other. If you are having problems getting it through, attach a safety pin to the front of the ribbon to help you guide it through.

Blanket stitched felt pouch

Take a piece of felt and draw a rectangle. Divide this into three sections lengthwise. Cut the top edge of the top section into a triangle shape. Fold the bottom section up so that it sits exactly over the second section. Blanket stitch the edges together to seal them then blanket stitch around the triangle shape at the top. Sew a button onto the middle of one side of the pouch shape. Cut a hole big enough for the button to go through on the triangle at the point where the button is directly underneath the triangle. Finish by blanket stitching the edge of the button hole.

Zipped circular case

Take a small zip (6" – 10", 15cm – 25cm) and bend it into a semi circular shape. Draw around this shape onto a piece of fabric then draw an identical semi circle below to create a large circle. Cut two of these from your fabric and two of these from your lining fabric. Take your zip and draw a rectangle that is as twice the length and width of the zip. Cut one of these in your fabric and one in the lining fabric. Sew one side of the fabric circle to the fabric length and do the same in the lining. Sew the zip to the other fabric circle with the lining underneath. Sew the other side of the zip to the lining and front piece of the long length. Turn the bag inside out and sew the lining of the bag together so that the stitches are underneath and will be hidden when the front of the bag is sewn up. Turn the bag around and, leaving a gap small enough to post the lining through, sew up the bottom of the bag so that the stitches will be on the inside. Turn the bag the right way round and top stitch the remaining hole.

Section Four

DO YOU KNOW HOW TO CAST?

Now you have met the runes, you have learnt how to chant them, and you have made your own set it is time to look into the ways to use them. The most well known use of the runes is for divination by casting and reading the runes to gain wisdom and make predictions. Using runes as talismans and to create bindrunes is very nearly as widespread and we will explore these in this section too. A far less well known use for the runes is galdr, magic, and spellcraft. We have already been introduced to the ways in which each rune can be used within galdr, but in this section we will concentrate on finding and using runes to meet specific requirements. We will also look at the ways in which you can combine galdr and bindrunes, and different ways that you can work with galdr.

Chapter 9

READING THE RUNES

The idea that runes can be used for divination has possibly come from Tacitus' description of throwing staves with symbols on in order to gain wisdom.[204] The popularisation of runes from the 1980s[205] onwards has meant that it is easy to pick up sets of rune stones and accompanying books showing you how to read the runes. Although this is a good start, it is worth remembering, that you should ultimately come up with your own system and that this may be an amalgamation of systems or it might be something completely different.

You may have tried other forms of divination, possibly Tarot Cards, I Ching, crystal ball, or palmistry. Some of these focus on the tool itself and the specifics of what certain things mean, whereas some of these are used as a tool in order for the reader to open up their own intuition and psychic abilities. The runes work with intuition in that one rune can have a number of possible meanings or messages it wants to give you, but that ultimately, the energy of the rune stays the same which means that its meaning within the reading won't stray too far from what it represents. This is not to say that you won't pick up brand new theories and ideas on certain runes while reading, nor does it assume that there are no psychic abilities or intuition involved, simply that the energy of the rune will be always have its distinctive energy.

KEEP YOUR NOTES CLOSE TO YOU

One thing that you will hear often when you learn the Tarot is that you should throw the book away and learn to read the cards without it. This is because the Tarot images encourage you to read in an intuitive way, and to use the cards in order to

---

204 The Germania, Tacitus, Penguin translation
205 Ralph Blum, Edred Thorsson, Freya Aswynn

focus and gain access to this ability. The runes need intuition and energy and understanding in order to read them, but the traditional stories and meanings of the runes as well as your previous thoughts about them can be extremely helpful while you are reading.

I would suggest that rather than use someone else's work on the runes you use your own notebook with your own theories and notes. This will almost certainly contain theories from books you have read and people you have known but will also contain a lot of your own ideas that you have built up from your personal work with the runes and from readings you have done.

FORMING THE RIGHT QUESTIONS

With all divination it is essential that you form your questions correctly. There are some theories that suggest that you should only ask the question once. This makes sense because you are undertaking a process of gaining knowledge from a source outside of everyday use. Whether you believe that the information comes from deity, the energies of the runes themselves, from your personal guardians or ancestors, or from the sub conscious, it seems a little impolite to ask the same question twice, as unless a fair amount of time has passed you are most likely to get the same answer.

In the same way, you might not want to ask the same question to different systems of divination or if you do, you might like to phrase it in a way that incorporates the understanding that you have already asked the question and that you are looking for more clarity or a different viewpoint. You can follow on from your reading with further questions on the same subject, breaking down the information given and using further readings to elaborate on areas of interest for you. You can also phrase your question differently if you realise that you have not been clear enough in your original query. Even with these tweaks you might find that repeated questioning throws out an *'idiot response'* (see below) from the runes.

Being specific

The key to getting your question correct is to be clear and precise. First of all, really think about the intent of your question. Often it is not immediately obvious what the question is. Just like when you work a spell, you need to think about the reason you want a certain thing. For example, asking whether or not you are going to get a new job is not necessarily the question that you are really asking. There are many different reasons for you wanting a new job – a more fulfilled life – financial stability. By asking about a new job you are forgetting these other needs. After all, to fulfil these needs, you don't necessarily need a job; you might find another way through. Of course it might be that in actuality you do want a job for a number of different reasons and the job is the whole of the question, but really think about whether this is the case. The same can be said for all kinds of questions.

Relationships, for example, are an area of questioning that often comes up. The needs that bring people to ask the runes for wisdom are often masked within the arena of *'I need a new partner'*. One solution to these needs can be a new partner; however, this is not always the only solution. Does the need come under companionship, sexual gratification, the want for children, intellectual companionship, or even personal gratification? (I.e. the way that having a partner can make you feel as though you are attractive/worthy).

READING FOR OTHER PEOPLE

When you are reading for other people it is difficult sometimes to have the time to fully explore their background and the background to the query. You can spend a small amount of time explaining the need for formulating the right question but you can't get to the bottom of their needs in the same way that you can your own. For this reason, the quickest and easiest way is to help them formulate the question. Ask them for the question that they want to ask and help them tailor it. For example, *'Will I move house?'* is not a helpful question because you can expect that at some time they are going to move house but that might be in ten or twenty years time. A few questions can help you to work out when they are planning to move house and whether the issue is one of buying or selling, moving from necessity or a question asked through curiosity.

When reading for other people it is important not to assume. Our experiences colour the way that we look at the world and something that is negative to someone is positive to another. Our experiences as well as previous readings we have done also mean that we might jump to a conclusion that is wrong simply because we have seen a similar situation in our lives or in a similar reading. Always ask the questioner what significance things might have. You can give a brief description of what that rune represents and then ask what that means to them.

Remember that the runes and you are helping the questioner to gain wisdom. This means that your role is to help them understand the spread but not to force your interpretation of it upon them. Let them work out what the runes are saying to them and it will help them to then be able to follow that up with how to transfer that into their lives.

Unless you have trained as a counsellor or similar, you need to remember that you are not one. The runes are a great source of wisdom and help to link you to that which is hidden, 'occult'. This can lead to incredibly powerful revelations. The trust we need to have is that these only occur when the timing is correct. This does not mean that it is an easy process.

Past traumas and personal realisations can be difficult to work through and as we have previously discussed, the runes can be blunt and to the point. If we are putting ourselves in an advisory position by reading a person's runes, we need to make sure that we take responsibility for suggesting that they find themselves someone to talk to if they need to. What we cannot take responsibility for is taking on something that we are not qualified to do. In the same way that you would insist that the questioner seeks medical advice for a medical problem, you need to encourage the questioner to seek further advice for an emotional problem if you feel it is necessary. In establishing whether this is needed, ask the following questions:

- Has the questioner ever received counselling before?
- Has the questioner had an abnormally high number of rune readings in a month?
- Is the questioner contacting many different psychics about the same problem?
- Is the questioner contacting you regularly outside of readings to ask your personal advice?

Remember that the size that you perceive their issues to be is not necessarily a true reflection of whether or not they need help so if you are concerned by their behaviour and you feel that your questioner needs some help managing their problems, don't be afraid to suggest it.

When to dare and when to keep silent

When reading runes for someone else you will sometimes need to use your own judgement on whether or not it is right to tell them everything that you see. Take in to account what you know about that person already (and more importantly, what you don't know about them) but let the runes guide you.

If knowledge is given to you in order to help with the reading, you will hopefully get an idea intuitively that you are not supposed to be voicing it. If you don't get this while it is coming to you, you might find that you get a real sense of dread or *'no'* when you go to voice it. Practise this with friends before you start reading for strangers to make sure you understand the messages. Knowledge that you are given for the reading but not supposed to voice can be from the past and present as well as the future. Don't fall into the trap of believing that voicing something from a questioner's past that has been unveiled to you to help with your understanding rather than for them will make them think that the reading is more truthful and that you are a better rune reader. Someone that is truly talented at something doesn't need to try and prove themselves and more importantly, it is likely to embarrass your questioner.

Knowledge that the runes are giving to the questioner is insistent. It forms in your mind in a positive manner and is repeated and repeated until it is voiced. Your own theories will be less insistent and you will be more questioning and reticent about them. This does not, in any way, make them invaluable, but you need to be aware that you are voicing them as your theories not as wisdom from the runes.

The 'idiot response'

The idiot response is something that comes up within divination when the question being asked is not being formulated correctly. It is important to learn to recognise this and to use it as a sign that you need to change or drop the question.

The idiot response comes in several different ways but invariably it means that the reading is giving out information that you know or believe to be incorrect in such an extreme way that the reading is completely unhelpful. This can be because almost every rune is face down and the ones that are face up seem to have no relevance to the question. It could also be that all the runes are the right way up, or it could be that the runes are coming out in order (i.e. futhark - Fehu, Uruz, Thurisaz, Ansuz, Raido, Kenaz) if you are working in a structured spread. The presence of only Ansuz within a reading, or the Ansuz rune falling out of the runes when you are shaking them and asking the question can also suggest that your question is not formulated correctly.

Chapter 10

CASTING THE RUNES

Take your rune set within your hands (or hold the bag in your hands with the runes in) and say your question. Think about the situation, but only say the question out loud once. Throw the runes (not too violently if they are breakable!) down. It doesn't matter what surface you are using but try not to lose any of them. Read the runes that have landed face up, and read them in combination with each other and based on their position in the spread.

Reading the runes in this way gives you access to lots of different information based on where the runes have fallen. Do they cross each other? Is any rune hidden? What way are the runes facing? How are they interacting with the runes around them? Which direction do you feel the narrative needs to be read (if any)? If you feel a real pull to any of the runes that are face down then take it as a sign that the extra information that rune is giving you needs to become part of the reading, albeit slightly later, and turn it over.

This is the easiest way of reading and gives the runes the greatest freedom to say what they need to, as well as giving you the greatest freedom to interpret what the runes are telling you. You can give this type of reading more structure by throwing your runes onto a cloth or a piece of paper onto which you have drawn segments that have different meanings.

THE 'TO DO LIST' READING

So called because it is based on the pre-printed *'to do'* lists that one of my past employers used to hand out. It divides a table into four areas:

	Urgent	Non Urgent
Important		
Non Important		

This design makes box one both urgent and important, box two important but not urgent, box three urgent but not important, and box four neither urgent or important. Where the runes land shows the urgency and importance of what they are telling us. You can adapt this layout to use any other terminology that fits. You could also use this for a more structured reading by taking a rune out and placing it into each of the four boxes.

THE TIME TARGET READING

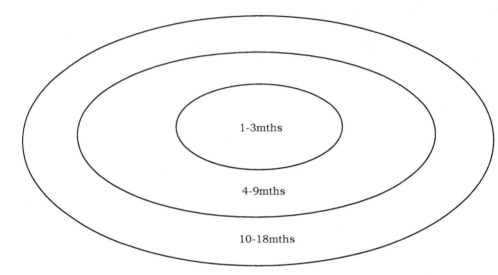

1-3mths

4-9mths

10-18mths

Use ovals one inside of each other to create a target. You could also use three different pieces of cloth, on top of each other. Specify a time that each of these represent. In my chart I have used 1–3 months, 4–9 months, and 10–18 months but it is just as easy to make them months or years. You can either not read any runes that fall outside of the chart, or you can read them as further away than the times specified.

THE NORNS READING

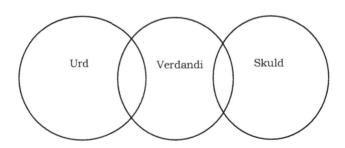

Urd

Verdandi

Skuld

The three Norns are Norse goddesses who weave the web of wyrd, and are said to control even the fate of the gods. Urd represents that which has been, Verdandi represents that which is, and Skuld represents that which should be, as the Norse view of the future was very much dependent on what was happening now in the present.

This reading uses the Norns to represent Past, Present, and Future, and has three circles that intercept each other on both sides. The runes can therefore fall within one of five positions:

- Urd, representing the past.
- Urd into Verdandi, just becoming past but still relevant;
- Verdandi, representing exactly the present;
- Verdandi into Skuld, representing present and very soon to be, and finally;
- Skuld representing the future.

You can also structure this reading by taking runes out of the bag individually for each position.

ONE RUNE READING

Reading one rune at a time can be helpful when you want to work quickly, or when you have limited space. If you are using a rune set that you carry round with you, a one rune reading can be a discreet way of working. Formulate your question with the bag of runes in your hand, and take out one rune to form your answer. If time and circumstances allows, and you are not able to work out why that rune came out, chant it and sense the energy and see how it is making you feel.

THE LOST RUNE READING

Occasionally, you go to read your runes and you realise that one is missing. This might be found fairly quickly, in which case, you have a one rune reading using the found rune which will be trying to signify something for you. Occasionally, this might be even more significant and you might need to work out what rune is missing and formulate what it is telling you and what you plan to do before the rune can be found. I had one set of runes in a lidded box that would fall off of the shelf every now and again (sometimes it would almost seem as though they leapt off without anyone being close to them). When picking up the runes, it would become clear that one or two would go missing and I would need to work out what they were telling me before I found them again. The telling sign was when I would line up the remainder of the runes and find it difficult to remember what rune was missing.

STRUCTURED READINGS

I am using the term 'structured' to describe a rune reading where the runes are placed blind from the bag into prearranged positions. This gives the reading more structure and less fluidity than the cast rune readings because you give each rune a specific role in the reading, for example – past, present, future. Many of the structured readings given in books are based on Tarot structures[206] such as the Celtic Cross. The use of the Celtic Cross spread in particular is a cause of disagreement within rune workers with the belief that there shouldn't be a reading spread referred to as Celtic.[207] Another popular structured spread to use is to position the runes into places representing each of the nine worlds.[208] Other ways to structure your reading would be to use a clock formation for the months of the year, or to use the seasons.

I have not given a lot of information about these more structured readings simply because I don't use them myself. I find that they are better suited to Tarot readings and that the runes themselves seem happier to speak when they are given more freedom to interact with each other.

---

206 Runes (the predictions library), Barret, 1995
207 Some authors have changed this to Odin's Cross
208 Leaves of Yggdrasil, Aswynn, 1988, & Rune Rede, Grimnisson, 2001

To Reverse or Not Reverse

You will by now have noted that I have not given any meanings for the runes being reversed. Many people will note, when reading, whether the rune is the right way up or upside down. This is to distinguish between the qualities of the rune and whether the positive qualities or the negative qualities are coming through for this reading giving the runes a shadow face.[209] I feel that this is unhelpful because the terms negative and positive are so subjective. What is a positive attribute to one person may be a negative attribute to another and different situations have different needs. The energy of each rune does not change dependant on whether it is upside down or the right way up. It is also difficult to read the reversed runes when you read the runes by casting them, because each rune interacts in such a fluid way that they land in a variety of different ways, which would mean that you would also need different meanings for the runes at different angles as well as reversed.

---

209 Grimnisson gives this the names 'shining stave' and 'shadow stave' in Rune Rede, 2001

Chapter 11

BINDRUNES

To make a bindrune you combine two or more runic sigils in order to create a new rune. This becomes a new sigil in its own right, which then contains the symbolism of all of the runes that you have put into it. Many of the runes from the later futharks look like a combination of two from the Elder Futhark. In fact, many of the runes in the third aett (Tyr's Aett) can also be considered to be bindrunes as they are a continuation of some in the first and second aetts.

To work with bindrunes you need to have a thorough understanding of the runes that you want to combine. This is because they can act differently depending on the runes that they are combined with. As when part of a bindrune, the energy of that particular rune can be heightened or dampened depending on which ones they are conjoined with. For example, Hagalaz, when combined with Berkana has less shocking and dramatic effects than it would when used alone because Berkana numbs the initial effect as well as speeding up the healing process once the lesson has been learned. The Hagalaz rune combined with the Thurisaz rune has the opposite effect and is a dramatic, sharp, shock with an explosive effect. By creating a bindrune you are able to tailor the effect that you want that sigil to have to a greater degree than by using just one rune.

Bindrunes can be a powerful way to create a sigil, however, a level of skill and understanding is needed to ensure that the runes you planned to appear in your bindrune are the only runes that you have appearing. It is very easy to create a bindrune that also ends up including runes that you didn't originally plan to include. Sometimes finding an extra rune is a help because you realise that the hijacking rune is appropriate and a positive addition. However, there will be occasions when the runes that you find accidently in your bindrune are going to have the opposite or an otherwise undesired effect within your sigil. This ultimately can make the bindrune unsuitable for task.

Intent may be the backbone of most magical practises, but with the runes, their individual energy will shine through and a rune used in the wrong context will make itself known, whether you intended it to or not. The Isa rune, being a single vertical line, appears in many of the other runes and therefore will appear in many of the bindrunes you create too. This might not be a problem. Remember that if the rune already has a vertical line within it then Isa is one way or another, already a part of that rune and therefore not going to add anything new to the bindrune. Where Isa becomes more of a concern is where the runes you are using do not have any vertical lines (for example using Jera and Kenaz). A bindrune containing Jera in particular may have a requirement (for example, growth or removal of blockages) that Isa might not be appropriate for.

Keep it simple. The more lines that you add to a bindrune, the more chance there is of accidently adding an extra rune. Take one rune as your focus and look at how to add the other runes into it using as few lines as possible. Be inventive. Change the angles of the rune, make it larger or smaller, or turn it upside down. Always keep in mind what changing these aspects of your rune could represent to the bindrune as a whole. Is it appropriate to turn the rune? Which direction does it face? How is it interacting with the other runes in the bindrune?

If you are struggling with a bindrune that you are finding difficult to remove additional non appropriate runes from you can do one of two things. The easiest of these is to try and take out the lines that are causing the non appropriate rune to appear, while trying to keep the general shape and sense of all of the runes within the bindrune. The second way is to use a runic wheel to create your bindrune.

When you are marking your bindrune, remember to charge the runes you put into it in the same way as you did your individual rune set by intoning the voice of each rune and using the sigil to channel the energy of the rune into the material you are marking onto.

USING RUNIC WHEELS TO CREATE BINDRUNES

A runic wheel can take several forms. In this version I use a wheel with eight spokes with three sets of horizontal lines marked onto the spokes in order to represent different runes. Each set of horizontal lines represents an aett, and the eight spokes represent the eight runes within each aett. Thus there is a place within the wheel for each of the Elder Futhark runes. The runic wheel for Fehu can be seen below:

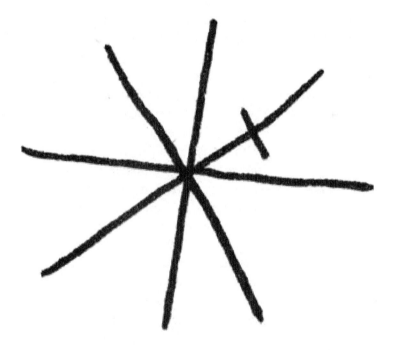

To mark a certain rune, figure out its position on the wheel and mark it on. The first aett runes are closest to the centre, the second aett in the middle, and the third aett furthest away from the centre. The first rune in the aett is the first spoke on the wheel, the second rune in the aett is the second spoke on the wheel, and so on. To create a bindrune using the runic wheel mark on the runes that you want to include within the bindrune (to represent one rune mark on just the one rune that you want). By using your bindrunes within runic wheels you are also making it slightly more difficult for someone to read and understand the runes you are using.

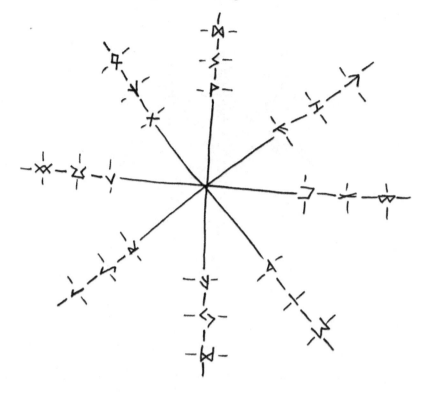

Another example of a runic wheel is the Aegishjalmur. This sigil is a very powerful bindrune which translates as 'the helmet of terror' or 'the helmet of awe' and is given the meaning of 'irresistibility' by the author Nigel Pennick.[210] It is accepted that this irresistibility refers to the wearer becoming invincible and undefeatable rather than being alluring. Perhaps considering Aegishjalmur as synonymous with awe and terror is more helpful than using the term irresistible. The Aegishjalmur is mentioned in the *Volsunga Saga*[211] as being a helmet that offers complete protection in battle for the wearer. It is a popular symbol for use within tattoos and talismans. The twenty-four points on the Aegishjalmur could be considered as the wearer

---

210 Rune Magic, Pennick, 1992
211 Poetic Edda, translation Carolyne Larrington

harnessing the power of all twenty-four runes. The marks on the outer side of the wheel are Algiz runes which invoke the terror.

The Aegishjalmur

Chapter 12

GALDR

For the purpose of this book, I am describing galdr as the use of runes for magic and spell craft.

Using the runes for galdr can be very powerful. Runes can be used as a system on their own, or they can be used in conjunction with another ritual. Typically, runes seem to represent a faster way of initiating a shift in consciousness or ritual space than many of the other ritual and religious techniques. Like the cultures that they grew from, the runes are direct and blunt. In the same way that modern Scandinavian languages use fewer words to get a point across than Latin based languages, runes use less language to achieve their effect than many of the modern magical systems. One or two runes chanted in the right way can sometimes replace a whole ritual that is designed to achieve the same result.

It has been discussed[212] that galdr was the male magic and that seidr (often referred to as witchcraft and shamanism within the Norse world) was the female magic. Some modern practitioners of galdr and seidr still argue that seidr is female and galdr is male. I like to distinguish between the two by saying that galdr is from the head and seidr is from the heart. Galdr is about language and intellect and uses words and symbols therefore it fits into the virtues that we traditionally consider to be male.

Seidr is about astral travel, using feelings, and speaking to the dead, therefore it fits in with the virtues that we traditionally consider to be female.

This is not to say that the use of runes within spellcraft can never be intuitive or work with astral travel. Nor does it assume that chanting and incantations are never used in seidr (the *Greenland Saga* for example features the *vardlokkur* – spirit

---

212 Nine Worlds of Seid-Magic, Blain, 2001

summoning song.)[213] Ronald Hutton[214] discusses the different kinds of paganism involved in the rebirth of spiritual thinking using the terms *'high magic'* and *'low magic'*. He explains high magic as organisations like the Golden Dawn and ritual magicians like Crowley. He explains low magic as cunning craft and local wise women. We can consider fitting galdr and seidr into this model with galdr representing the high magic and seidr representing the low magic.

Today runes have been used in spellcraft in a number of different ways. A lot of people use runes as protection, drawing them on themselves or on their homes. Each of the 24 runes has its own distinct energy and the majority of needs can be serviced with one or more of the runes in the Elder Futhark. Runes can be used for fertility, for childbirth, strength, healing, defence and attack, help with problems, money worries, and many other things.

Using the runes within galdr is mostly about chanting them for different effects. However, some of the suggestions for using the runes as galdr in this book also involve using the runic sigils and using the two together is very effective.

TALISMANS AND SIGILS

A talisman is something that is carried to bring you luck. A sigil is something that symbolically represents something else (often a name or a signature). Sigils can be drawings, music, or ritual gestures.[215] Often sigils are created for a magical purpose but they can also be a symbol (for example a number or a letter) that is being used to represent something else. Runes and bindrunes can be used in this way.

In almost every New Age shop and at almost every pagan event you will see rune symbols being sold or worn as jewellery or on key rings or other lucky charms. These are worn to bring the energy of the particular rune into the wearer. These

---

213 The Greenland Sagas, translated Gwynn Jones
214 Triumph of the Moon, Hutton, 1999
215 Visual Magick, Fries, 1992

talismans will often come with a one word explanation of what the rune represents and this description can be vastly different depending on who is selling them. This is another example of the mass market appeal of the runes, often being sold to people who have not worked in-depth with them.

Should you feel that you understand the energy of the rune you wish to wear enough, using the runes as talismans can be very advantageous. However, by wearing a rune as a talisman on a long-term basis you are entering into a different level of relationship with that energy which might cause an imbalance that could begin to manifest within your life. If you notice this happening and it is not the effect that you wanted, it might be time to remove your talisman.

You can also use runes as sigils on things like houses and cars to bring protection, or on objects of power that are required to do a certain job.

THE RUNIC ALPHABET

Modern usage of runes has also extended to using the runes as letters either to name something magically (i.e. a car, a house, a tool) or as a code. This perhaps is also evident in the use of runes in antiquity, as shown from archaeological finds.[216] Each rune in the Elder Futhark has a phonetic sound. Sometimes these sounds are easy to guess based on the shape of the rune as some runes are a similar shape to the English letters of the same sound, for example Fehu looks like an F and Hagalaz looks like an H. However, some are misleading. For example, Gebo looks like the English letter X but is pronounced 'g' as in 'go' and Wunjo looks like the English letter P but is pronounced 'v' as in 'van' (or more precisely is pronounced like the 'w' in 'wilkommen' in German).

---

216 Helrunar, Fries, 1993

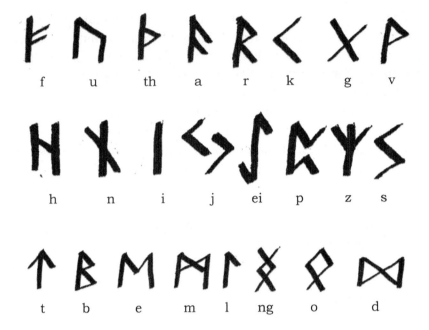

You will undoubtedly find slightly different pronunciations given for the phonetics of the runes depending on what author you read. For my chart I have used a combination of the phonetics given by Nigel Pennick[217] and R.V.W. Elliott.[218]

You can inscribe names into things like cars and weapons and magical tools but also onto other equipment that you might need to use. This works especially well with equipment that can be temperamental (like sewing machines). A word of warning however, computers don't seem to combine well with magic and runes. The Bluetooth symbol (sigil?) may well include runes, but in my experience, I have learnt over the years to avoid catastrophic hard drive crashes by separating my Norse magic and computers to different rooms.

A way to use the runes as letters while giving yourself a little more privacy is to spell out words using the runic wheels as letters.

217 Rune Magic, Pennick, 1992
218 Runes, Elliott, 1959

USING THE RUNES FOR MAGIC AND SPELL CRAFT

I have identified a few of the reasons that people might use runes. For each of these I have identified three runes which can be put together within galdr or bindrunes, and how these interact with each other, and more importantly, practical ways to go about doing so. Some of these (for example, healing,[219] childbirth,[220] and cursing[221]) are documented as being something that the runes were used for in antiquity. You might feel that some of these needs will never be appropriate for you, or you might feel that they are emergency situations. The runes have many uses, some of these will be day to day, but some will be substantial and life changing.

RUNIC PROTECTION

The three runes that are most appropriate for protection are Thurisaz, Eihwaz, and Algiz. Together these runes represent attack, support through other people, and fear. This gives us the unmetered attack of Thurisaz, the call of help and call to battle of Eihwaz, and the *'don't come close'* that Algiz gives out. Although they can all be used individually, the three together is effective. Algiz tempers the aggression of Thurisaz by creating an atmosphere that stops anything but the very foolish from getting close enough to be on the receiving end of the Thurisaz rune. Eihwaz adds to Algiz by taking away the aloneness that can make the energy feel stifling.

---

219 Egil's Saga
220 Women in Old Norse Society, Jochens, 1998
221 Egil's Saga

Bindrune for protection

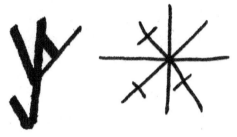

The protection bindrune uses a steady backbone which supports all three of the runes used and forms a strong Isa rune in an additional capacity. The Isa rune here supports and holds the three protection runes together which helps to ensure that Thurisaz is kept in check by the other two runes.

This bindrune is very balanced which ensures a balanced approach to protecting yourself and your property, which is important as often those of us who feel we need protecting are running on fear and adrenalin which causes us to act in an unbalanced way. The bindrune's shape is representative of an umbrella which in the modern context represents protection from the elements.

Galdr for protection

The most suitable use for the three runes for protection is as a bindrune marked onto your person or property or onto a talisman to carry around with you. Sometimes, however, it might not be appropriate to have the bindrune marked. In this case, you can use the same techniques to channel the rune into yourself or your property as you would for marking the bindrune but instead of marking the rune, draw the rune with your finger and visualise the energy of that rune assimilating in.

CHILDBIRTH

Pertho, Berkana, and Dagaz are the three runes which make up the childbirth trio. Used together they incorporate three of the worries of giving birth. Pertho swings the chance of fate within your favour which encourages a healthy birth and a healthy baby. Berkana calms both baby and mother, bringing peace and healing. Dagaz ensures that the labour is not too long, especially during the final stage of labour.

Bindrune for childbirth

The bindrune for childbirth uses the Berkana and Pertho runes as horizontal supports to the Dagaz rune. The Gebo rune which makes up a part of the Dagaz rune is clearly in evidence here offering the exchange. This rune is highly appropriate to childbirth in that it offers a gift for a sacrifice which sums up the sacrifice of pregnancy and birth in order to gain the newborn. The backbone of the Berkana rune is not drawn in order to keep the simplicity of the bindrune, but the Berkana rune is still very clearly represented here. This bindrune works best when created as a charm to be clutched while giving birth.

Galdr for childbirth

The three childbirth runes, Pertho, Berkana and Dagaz, work best when chanted individually at different stages of the birth. Although you can use all three together (see the bindrune above) within galdr each rune is best used when it is most appropriate.

The Pertho rune is used in order to invoke and protect the fate of the baby (as well as looking after the fate of the mother). Pertho marked onto the pregnant stomach ensures that things go the way that they need to in order to protect the futures of both mother and baby. Using the mucus plug (the 'show'), or the amniotic fluid from the broken waters to mark the Pertho rune across the stomach is incredibly powerful as it continues the protection that the womb offered the baby and is enriched with the protective maternal energy of the mother. You can also use Pertho at the point of birth to protect the newborn by marking the rune onto its skin using the amniotic fluid.

The Berkana rune works to calm and sooth. It also works to contain and ease pain. Both of these make it wonderful for childbirth. Birthing partners can mark Berkana on their palms and clasp them to the labouring mother while chanting the rune's voice and visualising the Berkana energy going from them through their palms and into the mother.

The Dagaz rune is used to speed up conclusions and new beginnings which makes it an excellent rune for either bringing on labour (when the mother is overdue) or for using in the final stage of labour when the mother is pushing. Dagaz can be chanted by the birthing partners and the mother at this final stage, or it can be chanted solely by the mother who focuses on the Dagaz rune while the birthing partners ease her pain with the Berkana rune.

BATTLE RUNES

The subject of battle runes or offensive runes often comes up. It should be noted that these are often confused with the cursing runes which work in a slightly different way. Perhaps it can be suggested that the battlefield is not such a large part of life anymore, but it is something that the runes have been used in conjunction with and therefore it feels wrong to leave out this bindrune. This bindrune can also be used as a focus for sports teams. The battle runes are Uruz, Thurisaz, and Eihwaz. Thurisaz is the attack, Eihwaz is the gathering of the front line cavalry, and Uruz gives you the bravery and strength of character to follow through with the fight.

Bindrune for battle

The battle bindrune holds the Thurisaz rune as the backbone. The Eihwaz rune in its positioning with the top mark at the same height as the thorn triangle forms a support for it, as does the Uruz rune which also adds balance. This bindrune is best when carved onto weaponry. Hagalaz can be added to this bindrune easily by extending the second vertical line. Hagalaz's addition will give a longer lasting effect to the attack but has the likelihood of offering a chance to learn from the experience.

Galdr for battle

The battle runes are mostly chanted. Thurisaz can be used as both a part of an attack or it can become a deterrent to an attack. Thurisaz used in conflict forms such a foreboding energy that it unnerves the attacker and gives you the upper hand. Uruz is used for bravery, as well as for strength and energy. As part of preparation it helps to focus and energise. Similarly, Eihwaz is used for strengthening the group bonds as well as making the chanter feel as though they have the advantage in number. Uruz and Eihwaz together can also be used as preparation by sports teams. Eihwaz strengthens the teams bonds and gives the team a confidence in their ability as a team. Uruz energises the individual and gives courage to push yourself and take chances.

FERTILITY

The three runes that are used for conception and fertility are Wunjo, Inguz, and Jera. These runes can be used for human fertility in order to help you conceive a child. They can also be used to conceive and create the seed that sparks other projects and help to ensure that they grow healthily. The idea behind this set of runes is that they work together for conception, therefore the galdr used with these works to create the new by using the sympathetic magic of conception and birthing. Be very clear on your intent if you plan to use this galdr to birth a new project.

Wunjo and Inguz are both connected with human sexuality, Wunjo representing the orgasm and sexual love, and Inguz representing the moment of conception. Jera adds the growth to encourage the healthy growth of the seed (whether that be within pregnancy or within the healthy growth of the project.

Bindrune for fertility

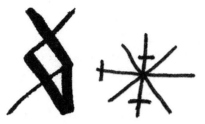

The bindrune for fertility focuses on the Inguz rune. The Jera rune is an intrinsic part of the Inguz rune considering that you can look on Inguz as an extension of Jera (the two halves of the Jera rune pushed in together becomes the Inguz rune). Therefore the Jera rune does not need to be added separately as it already appears as a part of the Inguz rune. The Wunjo sigil forms part of the bottom left stroke of the Inguz rune with the extra marking for the triangle being added as the one vertical line in the bindrune. This line being such a small part of the bindrune stops it becoming the strong backbone that would associate it with the Isa rune.

The positioning of the Wunjo rune means that this also does not become a backbone and Isa rune for the bindrune. The positioning of the Wunjo rune gives it the feel of it coming out of the Inguz rune which is a great symbolism for the joy of sexual union coming out of the of the rune that represents sexual union and conception. Within this bindrune there is also the Gebo rune and the Othala rune, but these are not a concern as these runes are inherent within the Inguz rune. Moreover the two Gebo runes representing exchange and sacrifice are a positive addition. In the same way, the ancestral and family links given by the Othala rune are also a positive addition to the bindrune.

Galdr for fertility

The fertility bindrune forms an important part within the fertility galdr. Working to conceive a child, the Inguz rune is marked onto the phallus using a combination of male and female sexual fluids. During sexual intercourse the Wunjo rune is chanted followed by Inguz at the point of orgasm. The bindrune is then marked onto the area of the womb using the combination of male and female sexual fluids.

To conceive a project or idea, you can use a version of this sympathetically (or 'in token'). Using the basis of the galdr for conception of a child (with sexual fluids for marking the runes optional!), use two pieces of paper, one representing the male and one the female. Mark the Inguz rune on one of these. Chant the Wunjo rune as you bring the pieces of paper together and the Inguz rune as you place the female paper (without the Inguz rune) on top of the male paper (with the Inguz rune). Mark the bindrune on the top (female) paper, tracing the outline of the Inguz rune if it is visible. Place a token (a coin, a shell, or something small which similarly represents the 'seed' of the project) inside the bindrune and leave for 24 hours to absorb the energy of the bindrune before using as a symbol of your new project manifest. You can finish by chanting the Jera rune over the bindrune and token to charge with successful growth.

RUNES AT HOME

The three runes which work together in order to protect the home and make it a safe and happy place to be are Fehu, Algiz, and Othala. Fehu brings the day to day wealth that brings home comforts like food and warmth. This gives the home everything that it needs in terms of repairs, warmth, and comfort and creates a comfortable environment within it. Algiz brings safety and protection. The choice of Algiz rather than the other runes associated with protection is because Algiz works to keep would be intruders away rather than to cause them harm. Othala creates a sense of homeliness and family to a house. The 'don't cross' feeling that sometimes comes with Algiz is not in evidence to those invited inside the house when it is tempered with Othala.

Bindrune for home

The bindrune for the home focuses on Algiz as the backbone and strength of the rune. An extra stroke is added below in order to create a Fehu rune. The Othala rune is added to the top of the Algiz, like a roof. The Othala rune is not fully drawn in this bindrune because of the additional meanings that the extra strokes give to the bindrune. To add the legs of Othala below the diamond would cause the additional rune of Nauthiz to be created. This works in direct opposition to the effect we are trying to achieve with the Fehu rune. To add the legs above the diamond gives the Othala rune an action of being upside down and pushing on or weighing down the Algiz and Fehu runes. To add the legs to the side causes an imbalance to an otherwise stable rune, and takes away from the intent that the home is a happy, stable, supported place to be.

The bindrune for the home can be marked anywhere within the home. If you were very creative you could use this bindrune (or create your own with your own personal needs) and use it as a stencil to stamp a pattern or border. If you didn't want to keep a bindrune in full view in your house you could mark it in the air or use something like water (on paintwork) that doesn't leave a mark.

Galdr for home

Moving into a new home or wanting to make your home feel like your own (if for any reason it doesn't) the best rune to use is always Othala. The best way to use Othala in this instance is to simply chant it and see the rune assimilate into the house. Chant the Fehu rune around things (like the boiler and radiators) that you want to keep working in order to ensure the house is comfortable. You could also chant it and see it assimilate into the kitchen to ensure that there is always plenty of food in the cupboards and the wealth needed to provide for that food. The Algiz rune is best used at the entrances. You can mark the Algiz rune physically at windows and doors or you could chant it while at the threshold and visualise the energy filling the threshold, stating the intent that only those you have invited in can pass.

If you are in the process of selling your house, you might want to leave the Algiz rune (and its *'don't cross'* feeling) and instead focus on the Othala rune. The Othala rune creates a feeling of being at home (and more importantly, of belonging) in everyone so it is a perfect rune to chant and assimilate into the energy of the house just before potential buyers come to view. It is the runic equivalent of baking bread. Remember to leave enough time so that you aren't loudly chanting runes as your potential buyers walk up the pathway!

CURSING

Cursing is another emotive subject that some may wonder the appropriateness of within a book of this kind. Indeed, the ethics of cursing could easily hold enough material for another book and because of this; I think it is important not to present an essay on personal magical ethics. However, to not include a section on cursing within this book is to ignore one of the widely known functions of the runes. If we look at the Sagas[222] we can see that cursing is one of areas that runes were described as being used for within antiquity. I present to you a discourse in the runes for cursing and allow you the decisions based on your own personal ethics.

The three runes that work together for cursing are Thurisaz, Hagalaz, and Nauthiz. Thurisaz strikes the blow that breaks through the barriers, Hagalaz brings the sharp energy that shakes and leaves you reeling, and the combination of Hagalaz and Nauthiz brings the inner pain that comes from understanding why your actions have made someone so angry.

<u>Bindrune for cursing</u>

The bindrune for cursing focuses on the Hagalaz rune which holds the central position within the rune. Thurisaz points inwards, breaking through the Hagalaz rune towards the Nauthiz rune which sits on the other vertical line of the Hagalaz rune. The Nauthiz rune strikes diagonally but its direction has the feeling of turning inwards towards Thurisaz. The cursing bindrune is introspective. The three runes sit in such a way that they turn into one another and the majority of the markings are inside the Hagalaz rune. This means that the Hagalaz rune is containing the effects of the curse which gives it less likelihood of rebounding on the sender. This is firstly because the Thurisaz is contained, but secondly because the energy given within the curse is used to consider and correct behaviours rather than in a destructive manner.

This bindrune should help the receiver to consider their actions and act accordingly which means that they are more likely to focus their energies introspectively and less likely to react within an aggressive and attacking manner. Using a

---

222 E.g.Egil's Saga, Penguin Classics

bindrune that encourages introspection means that the curse is aimed at pointing out unhelpful behaviour and encouraging a change in the receiver so that this behaviour is not repeated. This is far more beneficial to both parties than using a bindrune that simply breaks through barriers and attacks.

Galdr for cursing

To use the runes and galdr for cursing we can visit the world of seidr and feminine magic. Within Norse literature curses were often delivered astrally, that is a curse was delivered using astral projection to the bedside of the recipient, waking the recipient from their sleep and speaking the curse to them.[223] Delivering the three runes directly to the recipient via astral projection would be an incredibly effective way of delivering your runes personally, however, this is also potentially opening yourself to attack yourself while in a vulnerable state. This obviously should be not be attempted unless you are very sure of what you are doing. This technique is associated more closely with seidr and in my opinion, is perhaps one of the reasons why seidr was considered to be *ergi* (*'feminine'*, ergi is a term representing that a man is acting like a woman[224]). To deliver a curse remotely was far more cowardly than confronting someone face to face about their actions.

The order of the runes delivered in a chanted curse (whether that is done face to face or remotely) would be Thurisaz, Nauthiz, Hagalaz. Thurisaz is first because it breaks through the barriers that would automatically stop a curse from being able to get a hold. Nauthiz follows as it creates the right environment in order for someone to be able to learn from the lesson of Hagalaz. The Nauthiz rune means that the subconscious of the recipient is able to consider what it needs to change and adapt in order to learn the lessons of Hagalaz. The Hagalaz rune is the shock and the introspective thinking that allows the recipient to do the emotional and intellectual leg work that ensures that they learn the lessons that stop them

223 Leaves of Yggdrasil, Aswynn, 1988
224 Nine Worlds of Seid-Magic, Blain, 2001

repeating the behaviour that enlisted the need for the curse in the first place.

RUNES AND HEALING

Healing is something that should be considered with as much respect as cursing. Each situation needs to be taken individually and with the understanding that healing with galdr does not replace medical assistance. Similarly, part of putting together a healing programme is understanding diagnosis. An understanding of what needs to be done, coupled with sound medical advice, and taking the time to ask the runes for a divinatory reading to explain what needs doing, is key. Every healing is different and the intent needs to be thoroughly thought through in terms of what you are hoping to achieve from the healing and how realistic that is.

Remembering that each healing needs to be carefully considered on the right merit; the three best runes to use for healing are Uruz, Sowilo, and Berkana. Uruz works by giving strength and also bravery to endure and battle the illness or affliction. Sowilo works by giving the body the energy to heal itself. Berkana calms and has a numbing effect which can make it a good anaesthetic.

Bindrune for healing

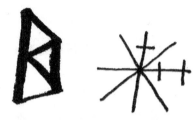

The bindrune for healing focuses on the Berkana rune. The Sowilo rune forms a part of the Berkana rune which means that it does not need to be added individually. The Uruz rune forms a roof for the bindrune with the second side of it joining the two triangles of the Berkana rune. Uruz stitches together the open side of Berkana. It also becomes a container, containing the dual energy of the Berkana and Sowilo runes in order to feed and contain their energy helping them achieve the results that they need to. Considering this bindrune in a slightly more modern context, the zig zag of the Berkana within the pillar of the Uruz rune is reminiscent of the striped *'blood and bandages'* signs that are on barber shops (barbers were responsible for surgery in Victorian Britain which is where the red and white signs originate).

Galdr for healing

Any magic or galdr that you do for healing needs to be carefully considered, as discussed in the first paragraph about healing with runes. The Berkana rune is used to calm and numb. It works similarly to an anaesthetic, calming the recipient and numbing the pain through focusing the mind on its energy. The Berkana rune works best when chanted for someone else but it is not impossible to use the Berkana rune on your own needs. Berkana is a pain relief but it is also a stress reliever which means that it works well on auto immune or anxiety related ailments.

The Uruz rune is the energy bank. Uruz works well with things like colds and flu's where you need the energy to get out of bed and carry on. It won't help your stuffy nose but it will get you out of bed. Chant the Uruz rune and see it assimilate into you. You could also mark it on yourself or mark it and intone it into food or water to give you strength.[225] The Uruz rune is the best rune for a person in pain or discomfort to chant as it not only gives them strength, but also bravery and courage. Uruz is a good rune to chant during operations performed under local anaesthetic. It is also a good rune to use when having dental surgery, although you won't be able to chant it in this instance. Instead you can visualise the Uruz rune being drawn in the air ahead of you, or you can clutch an Uruz charm.

The Sowilo rune helps the body to heal itself. It is a good rune to use to bring out bruising, to speed up the healing of broken bones, or to alleviate strains, sprains, and sore muscles. Mark the Sowilo rune onto the affected part (this doesn't have to be using something that will show) while intoning the Sowilo rune and visualising the energy going in. Use the way that Sowilo breaks down into three syllables to focus the chant as three syllables and three strokes. The Sowilo rune can even be marked onto the skin using heat or freeze spray.

CREATING A SACRED SPACE

When working with any kind of meditation, ritual, or magic, it is often helpful to create a sacred space to work within. From the primary information that we have on religious rites within Norse society there doesn't seem to be a set way of purifying and energising a space. However, with the popularisation of Western mystery traditions that use various rites to make the space they are working in sacred, some heathen authors have sought to create their own rites to designate the space they are working in

---

225 Leaves of Yggdrasil, Aswynn, 1988

as sacred. One of the most well known of these rites was originally suggested by Edred Thorsson in which he invokes a hammer in each of the four directions.[226] Nigel Pennick[227] gives us a different way to make our working space sacred based on the way that an enclosure was put up in Egil's Saga for use within a discussion.

Creating a sacred space using solely runes takes away the need to bring in any elements that have come from a separate tradition. It is a simple and effective way to purify and charge the space you are working in.   The best three runes to use are Kenaz, Laguz, and Othala. Kenaz clears the space of anything that might cause problems. Laguz continues this but works specifically on clearing away any emotional energy that will stop you concentrating. Othala creates a feeling of homeliness and calls the ancestors to you to bless the space and give it that sacred feeling.

Bindrune for creating a sacred space

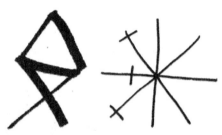

The bindrune for creating a sacred space focuses on the Othala rune. The Kenaz rune already forms a part of the Othala rune so doesn't need adding individually. Although there are lines that could be representative of the additional mark on the top of the Laguz rune, I have added it as a separate line which cuts horizontally across the diamond of the Othala rune. This effectively cuts into Othala making it look very different to the original Othala rune. By doing this the energy of Othala the homestead changes, the addition of Laguz, the rune of purification and cleansing, cutting through Othala changes the

---

226 Futhark, Thorsson, 1984
227 Practical Magic in the Northern Tradition, Pennick, 1989

energy into a cleansed space. This gives us the perfect symbolism to use when transforming a space.

Using this bindrune on a cloth or rug or piece of art within a room has the ability to help to change the energy of that room, helping it to take on the feeling of a sacred space. If, as many of us, you don't have a dedicated room that you only use for ritual (or a dedicated temple), then bringing out something with this bindrune on only when you are using the room as a ritual space will help to make wherever you are working feel sacred.

Galdr for creating a sacred space

Kenaz, Laguz, and Othala are chanted individually three times with each rune taking on a slightly different role. The Kenaz rune focuses on seeking out and clearing anything that doesn't belong there. Chant the Kenaz rune three times. With the first chant, visualise the space and use Kenaz to help notice if there is anything there energy or entity wise that concerns you. With the second chant, challenge that which was identified during your first chant and check its reactions. You might feel that it is perfectly fine staying where it is, or it might already decide to leave without any other action from you. On the third chant, visualise Kenaz banishing anything that you have decided is unwelcome.

Laguz is used to cleanse. I find that Laguz within this technique focuses on emotional energy both within the space and within the people in the room. It helps you to forget (or not think about) things that are going to distract you from the work that you need to do. Laguz is also chanted three times. While you chant the first Laguz concentrate on the space you are working in and visualise any emotional or energetic residue being neutralised. With the second Laguz chant, visualise yourself being cleansed and anything that you don't want to focus on being moved by a Laguz wave into another part of your consciousness to be parked for when you need to think about it again. On the third Laguz chant, visualise the energy of the Laguz rune washing through you and the space you are working in making everything clean and shiny.

Othala is used to bring in the right kind of energy to designate your space as sacred. On the first Othala chant, visualise the Othala energy assimilating into the space you are working in and marking it off from other areas. On the second Othala chant feel your intonation calling out to your ancestors and guides. On the third Othala rune, welcome the energies of your ancestors and your personal guides into the space you are working in.

SLEEP

If you are having problems sleeping (that aren't of a magical nature) then the three runes to use are Ansuz, Wunjo, and Berkana. Ansuz creates the mental calmness that allows you to understand what needs to be done and to stop you going over and over problems. Wunjo brings peace and general feeling of wellbeing. Berkana brings emotional peace and calmness.

Bindrune for sleep

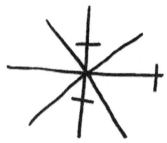

Berkana's emotional calmness and peace means that its place is as the focus of this bindrune. However, both Ansuz and Wunjo can already be found present within the bindrune of Berkana. This means that the best way to create a bindrune for helping you to sleep is to use the runic wheel or to simply use the Berkana rune. If you wanted to create a bindrune of these three runes, you would need to take the focus off of the Berkana rune and put it onto either the Ansuz rune (adding the Berkana rune to represent both Berkana and Wunjo to the top downward slope of the Ansuz rune) or onto the Wunjo rune (adding the downward slope of Ansuz onto the top of the Wunjo triangle and the two triangles of Berkana onto the bottom of the Wunjo triangle). Marking this bindrune onto yourself while you sleep or adding it under your pillow will help to challenge the factors that are stopping you from sleeping.

Galdr for sleep

The way to use these runes within galdr to help you to sleep is to chant them as part of your bedtime routine. Ansuz is used before you get into bed (perhaps while you are getting undressed/ dressed for bed) and it tackles the thoughts that could potentially swim around your mind looking for a resolution and stop you sleeping. The Ansuz rune in this situation helps you to identify what your subconscious is working on. By identifying these thoughts you are able to acknowledge them before your subconscious presents them to you and takes you away from the brink of sleep. By acknowledging them, you are able to consider when you will deal with them and give your mind a time the next day to bring these thoughts back to you.

Berkana and Wunjo work in very similar ways as they both work to bring you peace, calm, and happiness. Technically, using just one of these runes is adequate. Chant it when you are in bed and ready to sleep and it will relax you and help to stimulate the hormones that are released which help you to sleep. If you wanted to use both runes chant Wunjo followed by Berkana.

Chapter 13

CONCLUSION

Getting to know the energies of the runes is a long-term venture. To use them appropriately within sigils and galdr, it is important to meet with and understand the runes that you plan to use. Taking the runes out of context reduces the impact that they can have on the work you want to do with them. To fully harness and use the energy of a rune, you need to form a relationship with it. Every rune in the Elder Futhark (and the other futharks) comprises a separate energy so it is entirely possible to form a relationship with the runes one by one. You will find that certain runes speak to you more clearly than others and that this will change over the years.

Often you will find that the more someone learns about the runes, the less confident they feel working with them. It is often true that a little knowledge is a dangerous thing. Remember this when you are working with the runes. Make an effort to learn about the runes you want to use before you start using them for galdr or within charms and bindrunes. Most importantly, whatever you already know about the rune, be prepared that using that rune magically will inevitably teach you further lessons about it. If you are not prepared to learn the lessons of that rune, wait until you are to start working with it.

Whether you had no previous knowledge about the runes, only used the runes for divination, or have had a strong and beneficial relationship with the runes for many years, I hope that this book has introduced you to concepts, theories and ideas that are both new and useful to you. It is important to remember, however, that these theories are mostly just that, theories. I have no right and wrong answers, only experiences. Within your relationship with the runes the opinions and beliefs that matter are your own.

Hopefully, as well as new ways of using the runes for galdr, divination, and sigils, you will also have gained the inspiration that takes you further along your own journey towards your own experiments with bindrunes, magic, and wisdom.

BIBLIOGRAPHY AND SUGGESTED READING

Primary sources

The Poetic Edda, translation Carolyne Larrington, Oxford World Classics

Edda, Snorri Sturluson, Everyman

Egil's Saga

Eirik the Red and other Icelandic Sagas (often called the Vinland Sagas)

Heimskringla Saga (The Saga of King Harald)

Laexdala Saga

Njal's Saga, Penguin

Orkneyinga Saga

The Saga of the Volsungs

Ynglinga Saga

The Agricola and The Germania, Tacitus, Penguin

Modern rune study

Aswynn, Freya; Leaves of Yggdrasil; 1988 (reprinted as Northern Mysteries and Magic; 1990 & 1998)

Blum, Ralph; The Book of Runes; 1984

Fries, Jan; Helrunar; 1993

Grimnisson, Ruarik; Rune Rede; 2001

Kemble, J.M., & Griffiths, Bill; Anglo-Saxon Runes; 1991

Paxson, Diana; Taking up the Runes; 2005

Thorsson, Edred; Futhark; 1984

Secondary sources on Norse society, religion, and myth

Branston, Brian; The Lost Gods of England; 1974

Davidson, H.R. Ellis; Gods and Myths of Northern Europe; 1973

Elliott, R.W.V.; Runes: An Introduction; 1959

Holland, Kevin Crossley; The Penguin Book of Norse Myths; 1996

Jochens, Jenny; Women in Old Norse Society; 1998

Linsell, Tony, & Partridge, Brian; Anglo-Saxon Mythology, Migration, and Magic; 1994

Magnusson, Magnus; The Vikings; 2008

Pennick, Nigel; *Practical Magic in the Northern Tradition*; 1989
Welch, Lynda; *Goddess of the North*; 2001

Heathenry and Norse Paganism

Bates, Brian; *The Way of Wyrd*; 1983
Flowers, Stephen; *Galdrabok*; 1990
Gundarsson, Kveldulf; *Teutonic Religion*; 1993
Johnson, Nathan, & Wallis, Robert J.; *Galdrbok*; 2005
McGrath, Sheena; *Asyniur, Women's Mysteries in the Northern Tradition*; 1997
Paxson, Diana; *Essential Asatru*; 2007
Paxson, Diana; *Trance-Portation*; 2008
Sjoo, Monica; *The Norse Goddess*; 2000
Wallis, Robert J.; *Shamans/Neo Shamans*; 2003
Harner, Michael; *The Way of the Shaman*; 1982

INDEX

OTHER BOOKS BY AVALONIA

A COLLECTION OF MAGICAL SECRETS EDITED BY S SKINNER, D RANKINE

ARTEMIS – VIRGIN GODDESS OF THE SUN & MOON BY SORITA D'ESTE

BOTH SIDES OF HEAVEN EDITED BY SORITA D'ESTE, VARIOUS CONTRIBUTORS

CIRCLE OF FIRE BY SORITA D'ESTE AND DAVID RANKINE

CLIMBING THE TREE OF LIFE BY DAVID RANKINE

DEFENCES AGAINST THE WITCHES CRAFT BY JOHN CANARD

HEKA ANCIENT EGYPTIAN MAGIC & RITUAL BY DAVID RANKINE

HEKATE KEYS TO THE CROSSROADS EDITED BY SORITA D'ESTE, VARIOUS

HEKATE LIMINAL RITES BY SORITA D'ESTE AND DAVID RANKINE

HORNS OF POWER EDITED BY SORITA D'ESTE, VARIOUS CONTRIBUTORS

PRACTICAL ELEMENTAL MAGICK BY SORITA D'ESTE AND DAVID RANKINE

PRACTICAL PLANETARY MAGICK BY SORITA D'ESTE AND DAVID RANKINE

PRACTICAL QABALAH MAGICK BY SORITA D'ESTE AND DAVID RANKINE

PRIESTESSES PYTHONESSES & SIBYLS EDITED BY SORITA D'ESTE, VARIOUS

STELLAR MAGIC BY PAYAM NABARZ

THE BOOK OF TREASURE SPIRITS EDITED BY DAVID RANKINE

THE DIVINE STRUGGLE BY FREDERIC LAMOND

THE GUISES OF THE MORRIGAN BY SORITA D'ESTE AND DAVID RANKINE

THE ISLES OF THE MANY GODS BY SORITA D'ESTE AND DAVID RANKINE

TOWARDS THE WICCAN CIRCLE BY SORITA D'ESTE

VISIONS OF THE CAILLEACH BY SORITA D'ESTE AND DAVID RANKINE

WICCA MAGICAL BEGINNINGS BY SORITA D'ESTE AND DAVID RANKINE

WIZARDRY FOR THE UNINITIATED BY THEA FAYE

These and other esoteric titles are available from:

www.avaloniabooks.com
www.avaloniabooks.co.uk
Avalonia, BM Avalonia, London, WC1N 2XX, UK

CPSIA information can be obtained
at www.ICGtesting.com
Printed in the USA
BVOW06s0057171217
502998BV00005B/545/P

9 781905 297313